COLLECTION 8

My Hairiest Adventure
A Night in Terror Tower
The Cuckoo Clock of Doom

R.L. Stine

Hippo

Scholastic Children's Books,
Commonwealth House, 1–19 New Oxford Street, London WC1A lNU, UK
a division of Scholastic Ltd
London ~ New York ~ Toronto ~ Sydney ~ Auckland

First published in this edition by Scholastic Ltd, 1998

My Hairiest Adventure
First published in the USA by Scholastic Inc., 1994
First published in the UK by Scholastic Ltd, 1996
A Night in Terror Tower
The Cuckoo Clock of Doom
First published in the USA by Scholastic Inc., 1995
First published in the UK by Scholastic Ltd, 1996

Copyright © Parachute Press, Inc., 1994, 1995

GOOSEBUMPS is a trademark of Parachute Press, Inc.

ISBN 0 590 19750 9
All rights reserved

Typeset by Contour Typesetters, Southall, London
Printed by Cox & Wyman Ltd, Reading, Berks

10 9 8 7 6 5 4 3 2 1

CONTENTS

My Hairiest Adventure

Why were there so many stray dogs in my town?

And why did they always choose *me* to chase?

Did they wait quietly in the woods, watching people go by? Then did they whisper to each other, "See that blond kid? That's Larry Boyd—let's go get him!"?

I ran as fast as I could. But it's so hard to run when you're carrying a guitar case. It kept banging against my leg.

And I kept slipping in the snow.

The dogs were catching up. They were howling and barking, trying to scare me to death.

Well, it's working, guys! I thought. I'm scared. I'm plenty scared!

Dogs are supposed to sense when you're afraid of them. But I'm not usually afraid of dogs. In fact, I really like dogs.

I'm only afraid of dogs when there's a pack of them, running furiously at me, drooling hungrily, eager to tear me to tiny shreds. Like now.

Scrambling over the snow, I nearly toppled into a drift up to my knees. I glanced back. The dogs were gaining on me.

It isn't fair! I thought bitterly. They have four legs, and I only have two!

The big black dog with the evil black eyes was leading the pack, as usual. He had his lips pulled back in an angry snarl. He was close enough so that I could see his sharp, pointy teeth.

"Go home! Go home! Bad dogs! Go home!"

Why was I yelling at them? They didn't even *have* homes!

"Go home! Go home!"

My boots slipped in the snow, and the weight of my guitar case nearly pulled me over. Somehow I staggered forward, caught my balance, and kept moving.

My heart was pounding like crazy. And I felt as if I were burning up, even though it was about twelve degrees.

I squinted against the bright glare of the snow. I struggled to run faster, but my leg muscles were starting to cramp.

I don't stand a chance! I realized.

"Ow!" The heavy guitar case bounced against my side.

I glanced back. The dogs were leaping excitedly, making wide criss-crosses across the yards, howling and yelling, as they scrambled after me.

4

Moving closer. And closer.

"Go home! Bad dogs! Bad! Go home!"

Why me?

I'm a nice guy. Really. Ask anybody. They'll tell you—Larry Boyd is the nicest twelve-year-old kid in town!

So why did they always chase *me*?

The last time, I dived into a parked car and shut the door just as they pounced. But today, the dogs were too close. And the cars along the street were all snow-covered. By the time I got a car door open, the dogs would be having me for dessert!

I was only half a block from Lily's house. I could see it on the corner across the street. It was my only chance.

If I could get to Lily's house, I could—

"NOOOOOOOO!"

I slipped on a small rock, hidden under the snow. The guitar case flew from my hand and hit the snow with a soft *thud*.

I was down. Face down in the snow.

"They've got me this time," I moaned. "They've got me."

Everything went white.

I struggled to my knees, frantically brushing snow off my face with both hands.

The dogs barked hungrily.

"Scat! Get away! Get going!" Another voice. A familiar voice. "Get going, dogs! Get away!"

The barking grew softer.

I brushed the wet snow from my eyes. "Lily!" I cried happily. "How did *you* get here?"

She swung a heavy snow shovel in the dogs' direction. "Scat! Go away! Go!"

The growls turned to low whispers. The dogs backed up, started to retreat. The huge black dog with the black eyes lowered his head and loped slowly away. The others followed.

"Lily—they're *listening* to you!" I cried thankfully. I climbed slowly to my feet and brushed the snow off the front of my blue down parka.

"Of course," she replied, grinning. "I'm tough, Larry. I'm really tough."

6

Lily Vonn doesn't exactly look tough. She's twelve like me, but she looks younger. She's short and thin and kind of cute. She has chin-length blonde hair with a fringe that goes straight across her forehead.

The strange thing about Lily is her eyes. One is blue and one is green. No one can really believe she has two different colours—until they see them.

I brushed most of the snow off the front of my coat and the knees of my jeans. Lily handed me my guitar case. "Hope it's waterproof," she muttered.

I raised my eyes to the street. The dogs were barking wildly again, chasing a squirrel through several front gardens.

"I saw you from my window," Lily said as we started towards her house. "Why do they always chase after you?"

I shrugged. "I was just asking myself the same question," I told her. Our boots made crunching noises in the snow. Lily led the way. I stepped in her bootprints.

We waited for a car to move past, its tyres sliding on the slick road. Then we crossed the street and made our way up her driveway.

"How come you're late?" Lily asked.

"I had to help my dad shovel the drive," I replied. Some snow had caught inside my hood and was trickling down the back of my neck.

I shivered. I couldn't wait to get inside the house.

The others were all hanging out in Lily's living room. I waved hi to Manny, Jared and Kristina. Manny was down on his knees, fiddling with his guitar amp. It made a loud squeal, and everybody jumped.

Manny is tall and skinny and a bit goofy-looking, with a crooked smile and a mop of curly, black hair. Jared is twelve like the rest of us, but he looks eight. I don't think I've ever seen him without his black-and-silver Raiders cap on. Kristina is a little chubby. She has curly, carrot-coloured hair and wears glasses with blue plastic frames.

I tugged off my wet coat and hung it on a peg in the front hall. The house felt steamy and warm. I straightened my sweatshirt and joined the others.

Manny glanced up from his amp and laughed. "Hey, look—Larry's hair is messed up. Some-body take a picture!"

Everybody laughed.

They're always teasing me about my hair. Can I help it if I have really good hair? It's dark blond and wavy, and I wear it long.

"Hairy Larry!" Lily declared.

The other three laughed and then picked up the chant. "Hairy Larry! Hairy Larry! Hairy Larry!"

I made an angry face and swept my hand back through my hair, pushing it off my forehead. I could feel myself blushing.

I really don't like being teased. It always makes me angry, and I always blush.

I guess that's why Lily and my other friends tease me so much. They tease me about my hair, and about my big ears, and about anything else they can think of.

And I always get angry. And I always blush. Which makes them tease me even more.

"Hairy Larry! Hairy Larry! Hairy Larry!"

Great friends, huh?

Well, actually, they *are* great friends. We have a lot of fun together. The five of us have a band. This week, it's called The Geeks. Last week, we called ourselves The Spirit. We change the name a lot.

Lily has a gold coin that she wears on a chain around her neck. Her grandfather gave the coin to her. He told her it's real pirate gold.

So Lily wants to call our band Pirate Gold. But I don't think that's cool enough. And Manny, Jared and Kristina agree.

At least our name—The Geeks—is a lot cooler than Howie and the Shouters. That's the band who's challenging us in the big Battle of the Bands contest at school.

We still can't believe that Howie Hurwin named the band after himself! He's only the drummer. His stuck-up sister, Marissa, is the singer. "Why didn't you call it Marissa and the Shouters?" I asked him one day after school.

"Because Marissa doesn't rhyme with anything," he replied.

"Huh? What does Howie rhyme with?" I asked him.

"Zowie!" he said. Then he laughed and messed up my hair.

What a creep.

No one likes Howie or his sister. The Geeks can't wait to blow the Shouters off the stage.

"If only one of us played bass," Jared moaned as we tuned up.

"Or saxophone or trumpet or something," Kristina added, pulling out a couple of pink guitar picks from her open case.

"I think we sound great," Manny said, still down on the floor, fiddling with the cord to his amp. "Three guitars is a great sound. Especially when we put on the fuzztone and crank them all the way up."

Kristina, Manny and I all play guitar. Lily is the singer. And Jared plays a keyboard. His keyboard has a drum synthesizer with ten different rhythms on it. So we also have drums. Sort of.

As soon as Manny got his amp working, we tried to play a Rolling Stones song. Jared couldn't find the right drum rhythm on his synthesizer. So we played without it.

As soon as we finished, I shouted, "Let's start again!"

The others all groaned. "Larry, we sounded great!" Lily insisted. "We don't need to play it again."

"The rhythm was way off," I said.

"*You're* way off!" Manny exclaimed, making a face at me.

"Larry is a perfectionist," Kristina said. "Did you forget that, Manny?"

"How could I forget?" Manny groaned. "He never lets us finish one song!"

I could feel myself blushing again. "I just want to get it right," I told them.

Okay. Okay. Maybe I *am* a perfectionist. Is that a bad thing?

"The Battle of the Bands is in two weeks," I said. "We don't want to get onstage and embarrass ourselves, do we?"

I just *hate* being embarrassed. I hate it more than anything in the world. More than steamed broccoli!

We started playing again. Jared hit the saxophone button on his keyboard, and it sounded as if we had a saxophone. Manny took the first solo, and I took the second.

I messed up one chord. I wanted to start again.

11

But I knew they'd *murder* me if I stopped. So I kept on playing.

Lily's voice cracked on a high note. But she has such a sweet, tiny voice, it didn't sound too bad.

We played without taking a break for nearly two hours. It sounded pretty good. Whenever Jared found the right drum rhythm, it sounded *really* good.

After we put our instruments back in their cases, Lily suggested we go outside and mess around in the snow. The afternoon sun was still high in a shimmery blue sky. The thick blanket of snow sparkled in the golden sunlight.

We chased each other around the snow-covered evergreen shrubs in Lily's front garden. Manny crushed a big, wet snowball over Jared's Raiders cap. That started a snowball fight that lasted until we were all gasping for breath and laughing too hard to throw any more snow.

"Let's build a snowman," Lily suggested.

"Let's make it look like Larry," Kristina added. Her blue-framed glasses were completely steamed up.

"Whoever heard of a snowman with perfect blond hair?" Lily replied.

"Give me a break," I muttered.

They started to roll big balls of snow for the snowman's body. Jared shoved Manny over one of the big snowballs and tried to roll him up in the ball. But Manny was too heavy. The whole thing crumbled to powder under him.

While they worked on the snowman, I wandered down to the street. Something caught my eye at the kerb next door.

A pile of rubbish standing next to a metal bin.

I glanced up at the neighbours' house. I could see that it was being remodelled. The pile of rubbish at the kerb was waiting to be carted away.

I leaned over the side of the bin and began shuffling through the stuff. I love old junk. I can't help myself. I just love pawing through piles of old stuff.

Leaning into the bin, I shoved aside a stack of wall tiles and a balled-up shower curtain. Beneath a small, round shag rug, I found a white enamel medicine chest.

"Wow! This is cool!" I murmured to myself.

I pulled it up with both hands, moved away from the bin, and opened the chest. To my surprise, I found bottles and plastic tubes inside.

I started to examine them, moving them around with my hand, when an orange bottle caught my eye. "Hey, guys!" I shouted up to my friends. "Look what I've found!"

I carried the orange bottle back up to Lily's garden. "Hey, guys—look!" I called, waving the bottle.

No one looked up. Manny and Jared were struggling to lift one big snowball and set it on the other one to form the snowman's body. Lily was shouting encouragement. Kristina was wiping snow off her glasses with one of her gloves.

"Hey, Larry—what's that?" Kristina finally asked, putting her glasses back on. The others turned and saw the bottle in my hand.

I read the label to them: "INSTA-TAN. Rub on a dark suntan in minutes."

"Cool!" Manny declared. "Let's try it."

"Where did you find it?" Lily demanded. Her cheeks were bright red from the cold. There were white flecks of snow in her hair.

I pointed to the bin. "Your neighbours threw it out. The bottle is full," I announced.

14

"Let's try it!" Manny repeated, grinning his crooked grin.

"Yeah. Let's all go into school on Monday with dark suntans!" Kristina urged. "Can you see the look on Miss Shindling's face? We'll tell her we all went to Florida!"

"No! The Bahamas!" Lily declared. "We'll tell Howie Hurwin that The Geeks went to the Bahamas to practise!"

Everyone laughed.

"Do you think the stuff works?" Jared asked, adjusting his cap and staring at the bottle.

"It *has* to," Lily said. "They couldn't sell it if it didn't work." She grabbed the bottle from my hand. "It's nearly full. We can all get great tans. Come on. Let's do it. It'll be so cool!"

We all followed Lily back into the house, our boots crunching over the snow, our breath steaming up above our heads.

I pulled off my coat and tossed it on to the pile with the others. As I made my way into the living room, I began to have second thoughts. What if the stuff doesn't work? I asked myself. What if it turns us bright yellow or green instead of tan?

I'd be so totally embarrassed if I had to show up at school with bright green skin. I couldn't do it. I just couldn't. Even if it took months, I'd hide in my house—in my closet—till the stuff wore off.

The others didn't seem to be worried.

We jammed into the downstairs bathroom. Lily still had the bottle of INSTA-TAN. She twisted off the cap and poured a big glob of it into her hand. It was a creamy white liquid.

"Mmmmm. Smells nice," Lily reported, raising her hand to her face. "Very sweet-smelling."

She began rubbing it on her neck, then her cheeks, then her forehead. Tilting the bottle, she poured another big puddle into her palm. Then she rubbed the liquid over the backs of both hands.

Manny took the INSTA-TAN bottle next. He splashed a big glob of it into his hand. Then he started rubbing it all over his face.

"Feels cool and creamy," Kristina reported when her turn came. Jared went next. He practically emptied the bottle as he rubbed the stuff on his face and neck.

Finally it was my turn. I took the bottle and started to tilt it into my palm.

But something made me stop. I hesitated. I could see that the others were all watching me, waiting for me to splash the liquid all over my skin, too.

But, instead, I turned the bottle over and read the tiny print on the label.

And what I read made me gasp out loud.

"Larry, what's your problem?" Lily demanded. "Just pour a little in your hand and rub it on."

"But—but—but—" I sputtered.

"Do I look darker?" Kristina asked Lily. "Is it working?"

"Not yet," Lily told her. She turned back to me. "What's wrong, Larry?"

"The l-label," I stammered. "It says 'Do not use after February, 1991.'"

Everyone laughed. Their laughter rang off the tile walls in the narrow bathroom.

"It can't hurt you," Lily said, shaking her head. "So *what* if the stuff is a little old? That doesn't mean it will make your skin fall off!"

"Don't wimp out," Manny said, grabbing the bottle and tilting the top towards my hand. "Go ahead. Pour it. We've all done it, Larry. Now it's your turn."

"I think my skin is starting to tan," Kristina

17

said. She and Jared were admiring themselves in the mirror over the sink.

"Go ahead, Larry," Lily urged. "Those dates on the labels don't mean anything." She shoved my arm. "Put it on. What could happen?"

I could see that they were all staring at me now. My face grew hot, and I knew that I was blushing.

I didn't want them to call me a wimp. I didn't want to be the only one to chicken out. So I tilted the bottle down and poured the last sticky glob of the liquid into the palm of my hand.

Then I splashed it on to my face and rubbed it all over. I covered my face, my neck, and the back of my hands. It felt cool and creamy. And it did have a sweet smell, a little like my dad's aftershave.

The others cheered when I finished rubbing the cream in. "Way to go, Larry!" Jared clapped me on the back so hard, I nearly dropped the empty INSTA-TAN bottle.

We all pushed and shoved, struggling to get a good view of ourselves in the small medicine chest mirror. Manny gave Jared a hard shove and sent him sprawling into the shower.

"How long is it supposed to take?" Kristina asked. The bright ceiling light reflected off her glasses as she studied herself in the mirror.

"I don't think it's working at all," Lily said, letting out a disappointed sigh.

I studied the label again. "It says we should have a dark, good-looking tan almost instantly," I reported. I shook my head. "I knew this stuff was too old. I knew we shouldn't have—"

Manny's shrill scream cut off my words. We all turned to him and saw his horrified expression.

"My face!" Manny shrieked. "My face! It's falling off!"

He had his hands cupped. They trembled as he held them up. And I saw that he was holding a pale blob of his own skin!

"Ohhhh!" A weak moan escaped my lips.

The others stared down at Manny's hands in silent horror.

"My skin!" he groaned. "My skin!"

And then a grin burst out over his face, and he started to laugh.

As he held up his hand, I saw that it wasn't a piece of pale skin at all. It was a wet, wadded-up tissue.

Laughing his head off, Manny let the tissue float down to the bathroom floor.

"You jerk!" Lily cried angrily.

We all began shouting and shoving Manny. We pushed him into the shower. Lily reached for the knobs to turn on the water.

"No—stop!" Manny pleaded, laughing hard, struggling to break free. "Please! It was just a joke!"

Lily changed her mind and backed away. We all took final glances into the mirror as we paraded out of the bathroom.

No change. No tan. The stuff hadn't worked at all.

We grabbed our coats and hurried back outside to finish the snowman. I took the empty INSTA-TAN bottle with me and tossed it into the snow as Lily and Kristina rolled a snowball to make the head. Then they lifted it on to the snowman's body.

I found two dark stones for eyes. Manny grabbed Jared's Raiders cap and placed it on the snowman's head. It looked pretty good, but Jared quickly grabbed his cap back.

"It looks a lot like you, Manny," Jared said. "Except smarter."

We all laughed.

A strong gust of wind whipped around the side of the house. The wind toppled the snowman's head. It rolled off the body and crumbled to powder on the ground.

"Now it *really* looks like you!" Jared told Manny.

"Think fast!" Manny cried. He scooped up a big handful of snow and heaved it at Jared.

Jared tried to duck. But the snow poured over him. He instantly bent down, scooped up an even bigger pile of snow, and dropped it over Manny's head.

This started a long, funny, snowball fight among the five of us. Actually, it turned out

21

to be Lily and me against Manny, Jared, and Kristina.

The two of us held our own for a while. Lily is the fastest snowball maker I ever saw. She can make one and throw it in the time it takes me to bend down and start rolling the snow between my gloves.

The snowball fight quickly became a war. We weren't even bothering to make snowballs. We were just heaving big handfuls of snow at each other. And then we started rolling in the snow. And then we chased each other to the next garden, where the snow was fresh—and started another heavy-duty snowball fight.

What a great time! We were laughing and shouting, all breathing hard, all steaming hot despite the cold, swirling winds.

And then suddenly I felt sick.

I dropped to my knees, swallowing hard. The snow started to gleam brightly. Too brightly. The ground swayed and shook.

I felt *really* sick.

What's happening to me? I wondered.

Dr Murkin raised the long hypodermic needle. It gleamed in the light. A tiny droplet of green liquid spilled from the tip.

"Take a deep breath and hold it, Larry," the doctor instructed in his whispery voice. "This won't hurt."

He said the same words every time I had to see him.

I knew he was lying. The shot hurt. It hurt every time I got one, which was about every two weeks.

He grabbed my arm gently with his free hand. He leaned close to me, so close I could smell the peppermint mouthwash on his breath.

I took a deep breath and turned away. I could never bear to watch the long needle sink into my arm.

"Ow!" I let out a low cry as the needle punctured the skin.

Dr Murkin tightened his grip on my arm.

"That doesn't hurt much, does it?" he asked, his voice just above a whisper.

"Not too much," I groaned.

I glanced up at my mother. She was biting her lower lip, her face twisted in worry. She looked as if *she* were getting the shot!

Finally, I felt the needle slide out. Dr Murkin dabbed a cold, alcohol-soaked cotton wool ball against the puncture spot. "You'll be okay now," he said, patting my bare back. "You can put your shirt back on."

He turned and smiled reassuringly at my mother.

Dr Murkin is a very distinguished-looking man. I guess he's about fifty or so. He has straight white hair that he slicks down and brushes straight back. He has friendly blue eyes behind square-shaped, black glasses, and a warm smile.

Even though he lies when he says the shot won't hurt, I think he's a really good doctor, and I like him a lot. He always makes me feel better.

"Same old sweat gland problem," he told my mother, writing some notes in my file. "He got overheated. And we know that's not good—don't we, Larry?"

I muttered a reply.

I have a problem with my sweat glands. They don't work very well. I mean, I can't sweat. So when I get really overheated, I start to feel sick.

24

That's why I have to see Dr Murkin every two weeks. He gives me shots that make me feel better.

Our snowball battle was a lot of fun. But out in the snow and cold wind, I didn't even realize I was getting overheated.

That's why I started to feel weird.

"Do you feel better now?" my mum asked as we made our way out of the doctor's office.

I nodded. "Yeah. I'm okay," I told her. I stopped at the door and turned to face her. "Do I look any different, Mum?"

"Huh?" She narrowed her dark eyes at me. "Different? How?"

"Do I look like maybe I have a suntan or something?" I asked hopefully.

Her eyes studied my face. "I'm a little worried about you, Larry," she said quietly. "I want you to take a short nap when we get home. Okay?"

I guessed that meant I didn't look too tanned.

I *knew* that INSTA-TAN wouldn't work. The bottle was too old. And it probably didn't work even when it was new.

"It's hard to get a suntan in the winter," Mum commented as we headed across the snowy car park to the car.

Tell me about it, I thought, rolling my eyes.

Lily called me right after dinner. "I felt a bit sick, too," she admitted. "Are you okay?"

25

"Yeah, I'm fine," I replied. I held the cordless phone in one hand and flipped TV channels with the remote control in my other hand.

It's a bad habit of mine. Sometimes I flip channels for hours at a time and never really watch anything.

"Howie and Marissa walked by after you left," Lily said.

"Did you massacre them?" I asked eagerly. "Did you bury them in snowballs?"

Lily laughed. "No. We were all soaked and exhausted by the time Howie and Marissa showed up. We all just sort of stood there, shivering."

"Did Howie say anything about their band?" I asked.

"Yeah," Lily replied. "He said he's bought an Eric Clapton guitar book. He said he's learning some new songs that will blow us away."

"Howie should stick to drums. He is the worst guitar player in the world," I muttered. "When he plays, the guitar actually *squeaks*! I don't know how he does it. How do you make a guitar squeak?"

Lily laughed. "Marissa squeaks, too. But she calls it singing!"

We both laughed.

I cut my laughter short. "Do you think Howie and the Shouters are any good?"

"I don't know," Lily replied thoughtfully.

"Howie brags so much, you can't really believe him. He says they're good enough to make a CD. He says his dad wants them to make a demo tape so he can send it to all the big CD companies."

"Yeah. Sure," I muttered sarcastically. "We should sneak over to Howie's house some afternoon when they're all practising," I suggested. "We could listen at the window. Check them out."

"Marissa is actually a pretty good singer," Lily said. "She has a nice voice."

"But she's not as good as you," I said.

"Well, I think we're getting better," Lily commented. Then she added, "It's a shame we don't have a real drummer."

I agreed. "Jared's drum machine doesn't always play the same song we play!"

Lily and I talked about the Battle of the Bands a while longer. Then I said good night, turned off the phone, and sat down at my desk to start my homework.

I didn't finish until nearly ten. Yawning, I went downstairs to tell Mum and Dad I was going to sleep. Back upstairs, I changed into pyjamas and crossed the hall to the bathroom to brush my teeth.

Under the bright bathroom light, I studied my face in the mirror over the sink. No tan. My face stared back at me, as pale as ever.

I picked up my toothbrush and spread a small line of blue toothpaste on it.

I started to raise the toothbrush to my mouth—and then stopped.

"Hey—!" I cried out.

The toothbrush dropped into the sink as I gazed at the back of my hand.

At first I thought the hand was covered by a dark shadow.

But as I raised it closer to my face, I saw to my horror that it was no shadow.

I let out a loud gulping sound as I stared at the back of my hand.

It was covered by a patch of thick, black hair.

Staring down in shock, I shook the hand hard. I think I expected the black hair to fall off.

I grabbed at it with my other hand and tugged it.

"Ow!"

The hair really was growing from the back of my hand.

"How can this be?" I cried to myself. Holding the hand in the light, I struggled to stop it from trembling so that I could examine it.

The hair was nearly half an inch high. It was shiny and black. Very spiky. Very prickly. It felt kind of rough as I rubbed my other hand over it.

"Hairy Larry."

That stupid name Lily called me suddenly popped back into my head.

"Hairy Larry."

In the mirror I could see my face turning red. They'll call me Hairy Larry for the rest of my life, I thought unhappily, if they ever see this black hair growing out of my hand!

I *can't* let anyone see this! I told myself, feeling my chest tighten in panic. I *can't*! It would be so embarrassing!

I examined my left hand. It was as smooth and clear as ever.

"Thank goodness it's only on one hand!" I cried.

I tugged frantically at the patch of black hair again. I pulled at it until my hand ached. But the hair didn't come out.

My mouth suddenly felt dry. I gripped the edge of the sink with both hands, struggling to stop my entire body from trembling.

"What am I going to do?" I murmured.

Do I have to wear a glove for the rest of my life?

I can't let my friends see this. They'll call me Hairy Larry for ever. That's how I'll be known for the rest of my life!

A panicky sob escaped my throat.

Got to calm down, I warned myself. Got to think clearly.

I was gripping the sink so tightly, my hands ached. I lifted them, then rolled up both pyjama sleeves.

Were my arms covered in black hair, too?
No.

I let out a long sigh of relief.

The square patch of prickly hair on the back of

my right hand seemed to be the only hair that had grown.

What to do? What to do?

I could hear my parents climbing the stairs, on their way to their bedroom. Quickly, I closed the bathroom door and locked it.

"Larry—are you still up? I thought you went to bed," I heard my mum call from out in the hall.

"Just brushing my hair!" I called out.

I brush my hair every night before I go to bed.

I know it doesn't make any sense. I know it gets messed up the instant I put my head down on the pillow.

It's just a weird habit.

I raised my eyes to my hair. My dark blond hair, so soft and wavy.

So unlike the disgusting patch of spiky black hair on my hand.

I felt sick. My stomach hurtled up to my throat.

I forced back my feeling of nausea and pulled open the door to the medicine chest. My eyes slid desperately over the bottles and tubes.

Hair Remover. I searched for the words Hair Remover.

There *is* such a thing—isn't there?

Not in our medicine cabinet. I read every jar, every bottle. No Hair Remover.

I stared down at the black patch on my hand.

31

Had the hair grown a little bit? Or was I imagining it?

Another idea flashed into my mind.

I pulled down my dad's razor. On the bottom shelf of the medicine cabinet, I found a can of shaving cream.

I'll shave it all off, I decided. It will be easy.

I'd watched my dad shave a million times. There was nothing to it. I started the hot water running in the sink. I splashed some on to the back of my hand. Then I rubbed the bar of soap over the bristly black hair until it got all lathery.

My hands were wet and slippery, and the can of shaving cream nearly slid out of my grip. But I managed to push the top and spray a pile of white shaving cream on to the back of my hand.

I smoothed it over the ugly black hair. Then I picked up the razor in my left hand, held it under the hot water, the way I'd seen Dad do it.

And I started to shave. It was so hard to shave with my left hand.

The razor blade slid over the thick patch. The bristly hair came right off.

I watched it flow down the plughole.

Then I held my hand under the tap and let the water rinse away the rest of the shaving cream lather.

The water felt warm and soothing. I dried off my hand and then examined it carefully.

Smooth. Smooth and clean.

Not a trace of the disgusting black hair.

Feeling a lot better, I put my dad's razor and shaving cream back in the medicine chest. Then I crept across the hall to my bedroom.

Rubbing the back of my hand, enjoying its cool smoothness, I clicked off the ceiling light and climbed into bed.

My head sank heavily into the pillow. I yawned, suddenly feeling really sleepy.

What had caused that ugly hair to grow? The question had been nagging at me ever since I discovered it.

Was it the INSTA-TAN? Was it that old bottle of tanning lotion?

I wondered if any of my friends had grown hair, too? I had to giggle as I pictured Manny covered in hair, like a big gorilla.

But it wasn't funny. It was scary.

I rubbed my hand. Still smooth. The hair didn't seem to be growing back.

I yawned again, drifting to sleep.

Oh, no. I'm itchy, I suddenly realized, half-awake, half-asleep. My whole body feels itchy.

Is spiky black hair growing all over my body?

"Did you sleep?" Mum asked as I dragged myself into the kitchen for breakfast. "You look pale."

Dad lowered his newspaper to check me out. A white mug of coffee steamed in front of him. "He doesn't look pale to me," he muttered before returning to his newspaper.

"I slept okay," I said, sliding on to the stool at the breakfast counter. I studied my hand, keeping it under the counter just in case.

No hair. It looked perfectly smooth.

I had jumped out of bed the instant Mum called from downstairs. I turned on the light and studied my entire body in front of my mirror.

No black hair.

I was so happy, I felt like singing. I felt like hugging Mum and Dad and doing a dance on the breakfast table.

But that would be embarrassing.

So I happily ate my Frosted Flakes and drank

34

my orange juice.

Mum sat down beside Dad and started to crack open a hard-boiled egg. She had a hard-boiled egg every morning. But she threw away the yellow and only ate the white. She said she didn't want the cholesterol.

"Mum and Dad, I have to tell you something. I did a pretty stupid thing yesterday. I found an old bottle of a cream called INSTA-TAN in a bin. And my friends and I all rubbed it on ourselves. You know. So we'd have tans. But the date had run out on the bottle. And ... well ... last night, I suddenly grew some really gross black hair on the back of my hand."

That's what I *wanted* to say.

I wanted to tell them about it. I even opened my mouth to start telling them. But I couldn't do it.

I'd be so embarrassed.

They would just start yelling at me and telling me what a jerk I was. They'd probably drag me off to Dr Murkin and tell him what I had done. And then *he* would tell me how stupid I had been.

So I kept my mouth shut.

"You're awfully quiet this morning," Mum said, sliding a sliver of egg white into her mouth.

"Nothing much to talk about," I muttered.

I ran into Lily on the way to school. She had her coat collar pulled up and a red-and-blue wool ski

35

cap pulled down over her short blonde hair.

"It isn't *that* cold!" I said, jogging to catch up with her.

"Mum said it's going down to ten," Lily replied. "She made me bundle up."

The morning sun floated low over the houses, a red ball in the pale sky. The wind felt sharp. We leaned into it as we walked. A hard crust had formed over the snow, and our boots crunched loudly.

I took a deep breath. I decided to ask Lily the big question on my mind. "Lily," I started hesitantly. "Did any . . . uh . . . well . . . did any strange hair grow on the back of your hands last night?"

She stopped walking and stared at me. A solemn expression darkened her face. "Yes," she confessed in a hushed whisper.

"Huh?" I gasped. My heart skipped a beat. "You grew hair on your hand?"

Lily nodded grimly. She moved closer. Her blue eye and her green eye stared at me from under the wool ski cap.

"Hair grew on my hands," she whispered, her breath steaming up the cold air as she talked. "Then it grew on my arms, and my legs, and my back."

I let out a choked cry.

"Then my face changed into a wolf's face," Lily continued, still staring hard at me. "And I ran out to the woods and howled at the moon. Like this." She threw back her head and uttered a long, mournful howl.

"Then I found three people in the woods, and I *ate* them!" Lily declared. "Because I'm a *werewolf*!"

She growled at me and snapped her teeth. And then she burst out laughing.

I could feel my face turning red.

Lily gave me a hard, playful shove. I lost my balance and nearly fell on to my back.

She laughed even harder. "You *believed* me—didn't you, Larry!" she accused. "You actually believed that stupid story!"

"No way!" I cried. My face felt red-hot. "No way, Lily. Of *course* I didn't believe you!"

But I *had* believed her story. Up to the part where she said she ate three people.

Then I'd finally worked out that she was joking, that she was teasing me.

"Hairy Larry!" Lily chanted. "Hairy Larry!"

"Stop it!" I insisted angrily. "You're not funny, you know? You're not funny at all!"

"Well, *you* are!" she shot back. "Funny-looking!"

"Ha-ha," I replied sarcastically. I turned and crossed the street, taking long strides, trying to get away from her.

"Hairy Larry!" she called, chasing after me. "Hairy Larry!"

I slid on a patch of ice. I quickly caught my balance, but my backpack slid off my shoulder and dropped with a *thud* on to the street.

As I bent to pick it up, Lily stood over me. "Did *you* grow hair last night, Larry?" she demanded.

"Huh?" I pretended not to hear her.

"Did you grow hair on the back of your hand?

38

Is that why you asked me?" Lily asked, leaning over me.

"No way," I muttered. I hoisted the backpack on to my shoulder and started walking again. "No way," I repeated.

Lily laughed. "Are *you* a werewolf?"

I pretended to laugh, too. "No. I'm a vampire," I replied.

I wished I could tell Lily the truth. I really wanted to tell her about the patch of ugly hair.

But I knew she could never keep it a secret. I knew she would spread the story over the whole school. And then everyone I knew would call me Hairy Larry for the rest of my life!

I felt bad about lying to her. I mean, she *is* my best friend.

But what could I do?

We walked the rest of the way to school without saying much. I kept glancing over at Lily. She had the strangest smile on her face.

"Are you ready to present your book reports?" Miss Shindling asked.

The classroom erupted with sounds—chairs scraping, files being opened, papers being rustled, throats being cleared.

Standing in front of the entire class and reciting a book report makes everyone nervous. It makes me *very* nervous! I just hate having everyone stare at me.

And if I goof up a word or forget what I want to say next, I always turn bright red. And then everyone laughs and makes fun of me.

The night before, I had practised my book report standing in front of the mirror. And I had done pretty well. Only a few tiny mistakes.

Of course, I hadn't been nervous giving the report to myself in my room. Now, my knees were shaking—and I hadn't even been called on yet!

"Howie, would you give your report first?" Miss Shindling asked, motioning for Howie Hurwin to come to the front of the class.

"It's a shame to have the *best* go first!" Howie replied, grinning.

A few kids laughed. Other kids groaned.

I knew that Howie wasn't joking. He really thought he was the best at everything.

He stepped confidently to the front of the room. Howie is a big guy, sort of chubby, with thick, brown hair that he never brushes, and a big, round face with freckles on his cheeks.

He always has a smirk on his face. A stuck-up look that says, "I'm the best—and you're an insect."

He usually wears baggy faded denim jeans about five sizes too big, and a long-sleeved T-shirt with a shiny black jacket opened over it.

He held up the book he was reporting on. One of the Matt Christopher baseball books.

40

I groaned to myself. I knew in advance exactly what Howie was going to say: "I recommend this book to anyone who likes baseball."

That's how Howie always started his book reports. So boring!

But Howie always got As anyway. I never understood why Miss Shindling thinks he's so terrific.

Howie cleared his throat and grinned at Miss Shindling. Then he turned to the class and started his report in a loud, steady voice. "I recommend this book to anyone who likes baseball," he began.

Told you.

I yawned loudly. No one seemed to notice.

Howie droned on. "This is a very exciting book with a very good plot," he said. "If you like a lot of excitement, you'll like this book. Especially if you're a baseball fan."

I didn't hear the rest of it. I kept silently going over and over my own book report.

A few minutes later, when Miss Shindling announced, "Larry, you're next!" I almost didn't hear her.

I took a deep breath and climbed to my feet. *Stay cool, Larry*, I told myself. *You've practised and practised your report. There's nothing to be nervous about.*

Clearing my throat loudly, I started up the aisle to the front of the room. I was halfway up the aisle when Howie stuck out his foot.

I saw his big grin—but I didn't see his foot.

"Oh!" I cried out in surprise as I stumbled over it—and went sprawling on the floor.

The classroom exploded with laughter.

My heart pounding, I started to pull myself up.

But I stopped when I saw my hands.

Both of them were bristling with thick, black hair.

"Larry, are you okay?" I heard Miss Shindling call from her desk.

"Uh . . ." I was too stunned to answer.

"Larry, are you hurt?"

"Uh . . . well . . ." I couldn't speak at all. I couldn't move. I couldn't think.

Crouched on the floor, I stared in horror at my hairy hands.

Above me, I could hear kids still laughing about how Howie had tripped me. I glanced up to see the kid next to Howie slapping him a high-five.

Ha-ha. Very funny.

Usually, I'd be totally embarrassed. But I didn't have time to be embarrassed. I was too scared.

Had anyone seen my hairy hands?

Still down on the floor, I glanced quickly around the room.

No one was pointing in horror or crying out.

43

Maybe no one had caught a glimpse of them yet.

Quickly, I jammed both hands deep into my jeans pockets.

When I was sure that both hands were completely hidden, I climbed slowly to my feet.

"Look! Larry is blushing!" someone called from the back row. The room exploded with more laughter.

Of course, that made me blush even redder. But blushing wasn't exactly my biggest problem.

There was *no way* I could stand in front of the class with these two hairy hands. I'd rather die!

Without even thinking about it, I started hurrying back up the aisle to the classroom door. With my hands jammed into my jeans, it wasn't easy to walk fast.

"Larry—what's wrong?" Miss Shindling called from the front of the room. "Where are you going?"

"Uh ... I'll be right back," I managed to choke out.

"Are you sure you're okay?" the teacher asked.

"Yeah. Fine," I mumbled. "Be right back. Really."

I knew everyone was staring at me. But I didn't care. I just had to get out of there. I had to work out what to do about my hands.

As I reached the door, I heard Miss Shindling

scold Howie. "You could have hurt Larry. You shouldn't trip people, Howie. I've warned you before."

"But, Miss Shindling—it was an accident," Howie lied.

I slipped through the door. Into the long, empty hall.

I checked to make sure no one was around to see me. Then I pulled my hands from my pockets.

I had a dim hope that maybe my hands would be back to normal. But that hope vanished as soon as I raised them to the light.

Thick, black hair—nearly an inch high!—covered both hands. How could it grow so *fast*? I wondered.

The backs of my hands were hairy. And my palms were hairy, too. Hair poked up from the knuckles of my fingers. And clumps of black hair grew in the space *between* my fingers.

I rubbed my hands together, as if trying to rub the ugly hair away. But of course it didn't come off.

"Nooooooo. Please—noooooo!" I moaned out loud without realizing it.

What could I do?

I couldn't go back to class with these hairy monster hands. They would make everyone *sick*!

I would be embarrassed for the rest of my life. Whenever anyone would see me coming, they'd say, "Here comes Hairy Larry Boyd. Remember that day the black hair grew all over his hands?"

I'll run home, I decided. I'll get away from here.

No. How could I leave school in the middle of the morning? Miss Shindling was waiting for me to return and give my book report.

I stood frozen, my back against the tile wall, gazing at the hideous hands.

And I suddenly realized that I wasn't alone in the hallway.

I glanced up—and gasped when I saw Mr Fosburg, the principal.

He was carrying a stack of textbooks. But he had stopped a few feet away from me.

And he was staring in shock at my hairy hands.

46

I swung my hands down and tucked them behind my back.

But it was too late. Mr Fosburg had already seen them. His blue eyes narrowed as he studied me.

I shuddered.

What was he going to say? What was he going to do now?

"Is it too cold in the building?" the principal asked.

"Huh?" I replied. What was he asking?

I leaned back against my hands, pressing them against the wall. Even through my shirt, I could feel the prickly hair all over them.

"Should I have the heating turned up, Larry?" Mr Fosburg asked. "Is it too cold? Is that why you're wearing gloves to class?"

"G-gloves?" I stammered.

He thought I was wearing gloves!

"Yes. I ... uh ... was a little cold," I told him,

47

starting to feel a little better. "That's why I went to my locker. For gloves."

He stared at me thoughtfully. Then he turned and headed the other way, balancing the stack of textbooks in both hands. "I'll talk to the caretaker about it," he called back.

I breathed a sigh of relief as he disappeared around the corner. That had been a close call.

But he had given me a good idea. Gloves.

I hurried to my locker. Turning the dial on the combination lock felt strange with my hairy fingers. But I opened the locker easily and pulled my black leather gloves from the pockets of my parka.

A few seconds later, I stepped back into the classroom. Lily stood at the front of the class, giving her book report. She glanced at me curiously as I slid back into my seat.

When Lily finished, Miss Shindling called me to the front of the room. "Are you okay now, Larry?" she asked.

"Yes," I replied. "My . . . uh . . . hands were cold." I climbed out of my seat and stepped quickly to the front of the room.

Some kids started to giggle and point at my gloves. But I didn't care.

At least no one could see my hands with the ugly black fur sprouting all over them.

I took a deep breath and started my report. "The book I read is by Bruce Coville," I began.

48

"And I would recommend it to anyone who likes funny science fiction stories. . ."

After school, I hurried to my locker. I kept my head down and tried to avoid everyone.

I had worn the gloves all day. They were hot and uncomfortable. And they seemed to grow tighter and tighter.

I wondered if the black hair on my hands was growing. But I was afraid to take off the gloves to check it out.

I tugged on my parka and slung my backpack over one shoulder. I have to get out of here and think, I told myself.

A few steps from the next exit, I heard Lily calling my name. I turned and saw her chasing after me. She was wearing an oversized yellow sweater pulled down over bright green tights.

I kept walking. "Catch you later!" I called back to her. "I'm in a hurry."

But she came running up and stepped in front of me. "Aren't you coming to band practice?" she asked.

I was so upset about my hairy hands that I'd completely forgotten.

"It's at my house again this afternoon—remember?" Lily continued, walking backwards as I made my way to the doors.

"I—I can't," I stammered. "I don't feel very well."

49

That was the truth.

She stared hard at me. "What's your problem, Larry? How come you've been so weird all day?"

"I just don't feel well," I insisted. "Sorry about the practice. Can we do it tomorrow?"

"I suppose so," she replied. She said something else, but I didn't hear it. I pushed open the door and hurried out of the school.

I ran all the way home. The sun beamed down on the snow, making it gleam like silver. It was beautiful, but I couldn't enjoy it. I was lost in my own troubled thoughts.

Thinking about hair. Thick patches of black, spiky hair.

I burst into the house and tossed my backpack on to the floor. I started up the stairs to my room—but stopped when I heard Mum call my name.

I found her in the living room, on the chair by the front window. She had Jasper, our cat, in her lap and the cordless phone up to her ear. She said something into it, then lowered it as she raised her eyes to me.

"Larry, you're home early. Don't you have band practice?"

"Not today," I lied. "I have a lot of homework, so I came straight home." Another lie.

I didn't want to tell her the truth. I didn't want to tell her that I had rubbed INSTA-TAN all over myself and now I was sprouting disgusting black hair.

I didn't want to tell her. But it suddenly burst out of me. The whole story. I just couldn't hold it in any longer.

"Mum, you won't believe this," I started in a tiny, choked voice. "I'm growing hair, Mum. Really disgusting black hair. On my hands. You see, my friends and I—we found this old bottle of tanning lotion. And I know it was really stupid. But we all poured it on ourselves. I rubbed it all over my face, and hands, and neck. And now I'm growing hair, Mum. In school today, I looked down. And both of my hands were covered in black hair. I'm so embarrassed. And I'm scared, too. I'm really scared."

I was breathing hard as I finished the story. I had been staring down at the floor as I told it. But now I raised my eyes to see my mum's reaction.

What would she say? Could she help me?

I heard her mumble something. But I couldn't understand the words.

Then I realized that she wasn't talking to me.

She had the phone pressed to her ear, and she was talking into it.

Mum had gone back to her telephone conversation. She was concentrating so hard, she hadn't heard a word I had said!

I let out an annoyed groan. Then I spun around and hurried up the stairs to my room. I closed the door behind me and tore off the hot, uncomfortable gloves.

Jasper had run upstairs and perched on the window seat. She spent most of the day on the window seat in my room, staring down at the front garden.

As I tossed the gloves on to a chair, she turned to me. Her bright yellow eyes glowed happily.

I crossed the room and picked her up. Then I sat down on the window seat and hugged her.

52

"Jasper, you're the only real friend I have," I whispered, petting her back.

To my surprise, the cat let out a squawk, arched her back, and jumped to the floor. She ran halfway across the room, then turned back, her yellow eyes glaring at me.

It took me a few seconds to realize the problem. I held up my hands. "It's these hairy paws, isn't it, Jasper?" I said sadly. "They frightened you— didn't they?"

The cat tilted her head, as if trying to understand me.

"Well, they frighten me, too," I told her.

I jumped up and hurried across the hall to the bathroom. Once again, I pulled my dad's shaving equipment from the medicine cabinet.

I set to work, shaving off the thick hair.

It wasn't easy. Especially trying to shave off the tufts of hair that had grown in the spaces between my fingers. That hair was really hard to reach.

The hair was stiff and tough. Like the bristles on a hairbrush. I cut myself twice, on the palm and the back of my right hand.

As I rinsed the shaving cream off, I glanced down and saw Jasper staring up at me from the bathroom doorway. "Don't tell Mum and Dad," I whispered.

She blinked her yellow eyes and yawned.

The next morning, I woke up before Mum and

Dad. Most mornings, I lie in bed and wait for Mum to shout that it's time to get up.

But this morning I jumped out of bed, turned on all the lights, and stepped up to my mirror.

Would I find new hair?

I held up my hands and checked them out first. My eyes were still heavy from sleep. But I could see clearly that the hair had not grown back.

"Yes!" I cried happily.

The razor cuts on my right hand still hurt. But I didn't care. Both hands were smooth and hairless.

I turned them over and gazed at them for a long while. I was so glad that they looked normal.

I had dreamed about hair during the night. It had started out as spaghetti. In the dream, I was sitting in the kitchen, starting to eat a big plate of spaghetti.

But as I started to twirl the noodles on my fork, they instantly turned to hair. Long, black hairs.

I was twirling long, black hairs on to my fork. The plate was piled high with long strands of black hair.

Then I raised the forkful of hair to my mouth. I opened my mouth. I brought the hairy fork up closer, closer.

And then I woke up.

Yuck! What a disgusting dream.

54

I had felt really sick to my stomach. And it had been hard getting back to sleep.

Now at last it was morning, and I continued my inspection. I leaned over and checked my feet. Then my legs. No black clumps of hair.

No weird fur growing anywhere.

I guess it's safe to go to school, I told myself happily. But I'll be sure to keep my gloves handy.

After breakfast, I pulled on my coat, grabbed my backpack, and headed out of the house.

It was a bright, warm day. The snow glistened wetly. The sunshine had started to melt it. I stepped carefully around puddles of slush as I walked along the pavement.

I was feeling better. A lot better. In fact, I was feeling really good.

Then I turned and saw that pack of dogs. Snarling dogs. Heading right for me.

13

My heart jumped up to my throat. The dogs were running full speed, their heads bobbing up and down, their eyes trained on me. They barked and growled furiously with each bounding step.

My legs suddenly felt as if they weighed a thousand pounds. But I whirled around and forced myself to run.

If they catch me, they'll tear me to pieces! I told myself. They must smell Jasper on me, I decided. That's why they always chase me.

I loved my cat. But why did she have to get me in so much trouble?

Who owned these vicious dogs, anyway? Why were they allowed to run wild like this?

Questions, questions. They flew through my mind as I ran. Across front gardens. Then across the street.

A car horn blared. I heard the squeal of brakes.

A car skidded towards the opposite kerb.

I had forgotten to check the traffic before I crossed.

"Sorry!" I called. And kept running.

A sharp pain in my side forced me to slow down. I turned and saw the yapping dogs racing steadily towards me. They crossed the street and kept moving over the snowy ground. Closer. Closer.

"Hey, Larry!" Two kids stepped on to the pavement ahead of me.

"Run!" I screamed breathlessly. "The dogs—"

But Lily and Jared didn't move.

I stepped up to them, holding my side. It ached so hard, I could barely breathe.

Lily turned to stare down the dogs, as she had done before. Jared stepped up to meet them. All three of us watched the dogs approach.

Seeing the three of us standing together, the dogs slowed to a stop. The snarls and growls stopped instantly. They stared back at us uncertainly. They were panting hard, their tongues drooping down nearly to the snow.

"Go home!" Lily shouted. She stamped her shoe hard on the pavement.

The big black dog, the leader, uttered a low whimper and hung his head.

"Go home! Go home!" All three of us chanted.

The pain in my side started to fade. I felt a little better. The dogs weren't going to attack, I could see. They didn't want to tangle with all three of us.

They turned and started to trot away, following the big black dog.

Suddenly Jared started to laugh. "Look at that one!" he cried. He pointed to a long, scrawny dog with black, curly fur.

"What's so funny about that one?" I demanded.

"He looks just like Manny!" Jared declared.

Lily started to laugh. "You're right! He does!"

All three of us laughed. The dog had Manny's curly hair. And he had Manny's dark, soulful eyes.

"Come on. We'll be late," Lily said. She kicked a hard clump of snow off the pavement. Jared and I followed her towards school.

"Why were those dogs chasing you?" Jared asked.

"I think because they smelled my cat," I replied.

"Those dogs are mean," Lily said, a few steps ahead of us. "They shouldn't let them run wild like that."

"Tell me about it," I replied, rolling my eyes.

A sharp gust of wind nearly blew us backwards over the slippery pavement. Jared's Raiders cap went flying into the street. An estate car rumbled past, nearly running it over.

Jared darted into the street and snatched the

58

cap back. "I'll be glad when winter is over," he muttered.

We met Kristina in front of the school. Her red hair blew wildly around her head in the swirling wind. "Do we have band practice this afternoon?" she asked. She was chewing a Snickers bar.

"Great breakfast," I said sarcastically.

"Mum didn't have time to make eggs," Kristina replied, chewing.

"Yes. Practice at my house," Lily said. "We've got to get to work, guys. We don't want Howie to win the contest."

Kristina turned to me. "Where were you yesterday?"

"I . . . uh . . . didn't feel too well," I replied.

That reminded me of the INSTA-TAN lotion. Were any of my friends growing hair, too, because of that suntan gunk? I had to know. I had to ask.

But if they weren't growing hair—if I was the only one—then I'd be totally embarrassed.

"Uh . . . remember that INSTA-TAN stuff?" I asked quietly.

"Great stuff," Jared replied. "I think it made me paler!"

Kristina laughed. "It didn't work at all. You were right, Larry. That bottle was too old."

"Look at us," Lily added. "We're all as pale as the snow. That stuff didn't do anything."

But are you growing weird black patches of hair now?

That's what I was dying to ask.

But none of them said anything about growing hair.

Were they like me? Were they too embarrassed to admit it?

Or was I the only one?

I took a deep breath. Should I ask? Should I ask if anyone was sprouting hair?

I opened my mouth to ask. But I stopped when I realized that the subject had changed. They were talking about our band again.

"Can you bring your amp to my house?" Lily asked Kristina. "Manny will bring his. But it only has jacks to plug in two guitars."

"Maybe I can bring mine—" I started to say.

But a gust of wind blew my parka hood back.

I reached up to pull the hood back on my head.

But my hand brushed the back of my neck—and I gasped.

The back of my neck was covered with thick hair.

"Larry—what's wrong?" Lily demanded.

"Uh . . . uh . . ." I couldn't speak.

"What's wrong with your scarf?" Jared asked. "Is it too tight?" He tugged at the wool scarf around my neck.

The scratchy scarf my mum made me wear because my great-aunt Hildy had knitted it.

I had forgotten I was wearing it. When my hand brushed against it, I'd thought . . .

"You looked scared to death!" Lily exclaimed. "Are you okay, Larry?"

I nodded. "Yeah. I'm okay," I muttered, feeling my face go red. "The scarf was choking me, I guess." What a lame lie.

But I had to say *something*. I couldn't say that I had mistakenly thought that my neck had sprouted fur!

Larry, you've got to stop thinking about hair! I scolded myself. If you don't, you'll drive yourself crazy!

I shivered. "Let's go inside," I said, wrapping the wool scarf tightly around my neck.

I hurried to the boys' room to brush my hair before the bell rang. Gazing at my wavy, blond hair in the mirror as I brushed it, I had a horrifying thought.

What if my real hair suddenly fell out? And the horrible, prickly black hair grew in its place?

What if I woke up one morning, and my entire head was covered in the disgusting black fur?

I took a long look at myself in the mirror. Someone had smeared soap over the glass, and my reflection appeared to stare back through hazy, white streaks.

"Shape up," I told myself.

I pointed a finger at my reflection. A smooth, hairless finger.

"Stop thinking about hair, Larry," I instructed my reflection. "Stop thinking about it. You're going to be okay."

The INSTA-TAN lotion has worn off, I decided.

It had been several days since my friends and I had splashed it on ourselves. I had taken at least three showers and two baths.

It's worn off, I told myself. It's all gone. Stop worrying about it.

I took one last glance at my hair. It was getting pretty long, but I liked it that way. I

62

liked brushing the sides back over my ears.

Maybe I'll let it grow *really* long, I thought. I tucked the hairbrush into my backpack and headed to class.

I had a pretty good day until Miss Shindling handed back the history term papers.

It wasn't the grade that upset me. She gave me a ninety-four, which is really good. I knew that Lily would probably brag that she got a ninety-eight or a ninety-nine. But Lily was great at writing.

A ninety-four was really excellent for me.

The grade made me happy. But when I flipped through the pages, glancing over Miss Shindling's comments on my writing, I found a black hair on page three.

Was it *my* black hair? I wondered. Was it one of the disgusting black hairs that had sprouted on my hands?

Or was it Miss Shindling's? Miss Shindling had short, straight black hair. It *could* be one of hers.

Or else . . .

I squinted at the hair, afraid to touch it.

I knew I was starting to get weird. I knew I had made a solemn vow that I was going to stop thinking about hair.

But I couldn't help it.

Seeing this one, stubby, little black hair stuck

to the third page of my term paper gave me the shudders. Finally, I raised the term paper close to my face—and blew the hair away.

I didn't hear a word Miss Shindling said for the rest of the class. I was glad when the bell rang and it was time to go to gym.

It will feel good to run around and get some exercise, I decided.

"Basketball today!" Coach Rafferty shouted as we filed into the brightly lit gym. "Basketball today! Change into your shorts! Come on—hustle!"

I usually don't like basketball that much. There's so much running back and forth. Back and forth the entire length of the floor. Also, I don't have a very good shooting eye. And I get really embarrassed when a teammate passes me the ball and I miss an easy shot.

But, today, basketball sounded just right. A chance to run and get rid of a lot of my nervous energy.

I followed the other guys in the locker room. We all opened our gym lockers and pulled out our shorts and T-shirts.

At the end of the row of lockers, Howie Hurwin kept shouting, "In your face! In your face!"

Another guy snapped a towel at Howie.

Serves him right, I thought. Howie is such a jerk.

"In your face!" I heard Howie chant. Someone shouted to him to shut up.

"In your face, man! In your face!"

I sat down on the bench and pulled off my trainers. Then I stood up and started to pull off my jeans.

I stopped when I got the jeans about halfway down.

I stopped and let out a low cry when I saw my knees.

Bushy clumps of furry black hair had sprouted from both knees.

"How come you kept your jeans on in gym?" Jared asked.

"Huh?" His question caught me by surprise. It was the next day, and we were walking along the slushy sidewalks, lugging our instruments to Lily's house for another band practice.

"You refused to change into gym shorts, remember?" Jared said, swinging his keyboard case at his side.

"I . . . was just cold," I told him. "My legs got cold. That's all. I don't know why Coach Rafferty gave me such a hard time."

Jared laughed. "Rafferty nearly swallowed his whistle when you sank that three-point jump shot from mid-court!"

I laughed, too. I am the worst shot in school. But I was so crazed about my hairy knees, so totally *pumped*, that I played better than I'd ever played in my life.

"Maybe you should wear jeans *all* the time!"

Coach Rafferty had joked.

But, of course, it was no joke.

I ran all the way home after school and spent nearly half an hour locked in the upstairs bathroom, shaving the clumps of black hair off my knees.

When I finally finished, both knees were red and sore. But at least they were smooth again.

I spent the rest of the afternoon closed up in my room, thinking hard about what was happening to me. Unfortunately, all I came up with were questions. Dozens of questions.

But no answers.

Sprawled on my stomach on top of the bed, my knees throbbed as I thought. Why did my knees grow hair? I asked myself. I didn't spread any INSTA-TAN on my knees. So why did the ugly black hair sprout there?

Had the INSTA-TAN worked itself into my system? Had the strange liquid seeped into my pores? Had it spread through my entire body?

Was I going to turn into some kind of big, hairy creature? Was I soon going to look like King Kong or something?

Questions—but no answers.

The questions still troubled me as I crossed the street with Jared, and Lily's white-frame house came into view on the corner.

The sun beamed down above the two bare maple trees that leaned over Lily's driveway.

The air felt warm, almost like spring. The snow had melted a lot in one day. Patches of wet grass poked up through the white.

In the yard across the street from Lily's house, a half-melted snowman looked sad and droopy. My trainers splashed through the slushy puddles as Jared and I carried our instruments up the driveway.

Lily opened the door for us. She and Kristina had already been practising. Lily was wearing a bright red-and-blue ski sweater pulled down over pale blue leggings. Kristina wore faded jeans and a green-and-gold Notre Dame sweat-shirt.

"Where's Manny?" Lily asked, closing the front door behind Jared and me.

"Haven't seen him," I replied, scraping my wet trainers on the floor mat. "Isn't he here?"

"He wasn't in school again today," Kristina reported.

"We've got to get serious," Lily said, biting her lower lip. "Did you talk to Howie today? Did he tell you what his dad bought him?"

"A new synthesizer?" I replied, bending to open my guitar case. "Yeah. Howie told me all about it. He says it can sound like an entire orchestra."

"Who wants to sound like an orchestra?" Jared asked. He had a wet leaf stuck to his shoe. He pulled it off, but then didn't know where to

68

throw it away. So he jammed it in his jeans pocket.

"If Howie sounds like an orchestra, and we sound like three guitars and a kiddie keyboard, we're in major trouble," Lily warned.

"It's *not* a kiddie keyboard!" Jared protested.

I laughed. "Just because you wind a crank at the side of it doesn't make it a kiddie keyboard!"

"It's small—but it has all the notes," Jared insisted. He set the keyboard on the coffee table and bent down to plug it in.

"Let's stop messing around and get to work," Kristina said, moving her fingers over the frets of her shiny red Gibson. "What song do you want to practise first?"

"How can we practise without Manny?" I asked. "I mean, what's the point?"

"I tried calling him," Lily said. "But his phone is messed up or something. It didn't even ring."

"Let's go to his house and get him," I suggested.

"Yeah. Good idea!" Kristina agreed.

All four of us started for the front entryway to get our coats. But Lily stopped at the door. "Larry and I will go," she announced to Kristina. "You and Jared should stay and practise. Why should we all go?"

"Okay," Jared agreed quickly. "Besides, someone should be here in case Manny shows up."

With that settled, Lily and I pulled on our

coats and headed out of the front door. Lily's Doc Martens splashed through a wide puddle as we made our way along the pavement.

"I hate it when the snow gets all grey and slushy," she said. "Listen. All you can hear is dripping. Water dripping from the trees, dripping from the houses."

She stuck out her arm to block my path and stop me from walking. We listened in silence to the dripping sounds.

"It's deafening—isn't it?" Lily asked, smiling. The sunlight reflected in her eyes. One blue eye, one green eye.

"Deafening," I repeated. Lily can be pretty weird sometimes. She once told me that she writes poetry. Long poems about nature. But she's never shown any of them to me.

We trudged through the slush. The sun felt warm on my face. I unzipped my parka.

Manny's house came into view as we turned the corner. Manny lives in a square-shaped brick house on top of a hill. It's a great sledding hill. There were two little kids sledding down it now on blue plastic discs. They were going pretty slow since most of the snow had melted.

We walked past them and made our way up to Manny's front doorstep. Lily rang the door-bell, and I knocked. "Hey, Manny—open up!" I shouted.

No reply.

No sounds at all. Just the *drip drip drip* of water from the gutter.

"Hey, Manny!" I called. We rang and knocked again.

"No one home," Lily said quietly. She stepped off the doorstep and moved to the front window. Edging up on tiptoes, she tried to peer in.

"See anything?" I called.

She shook her head. "No. The sun is reflecting on the glass. It looks dark inside."

"There's no car in the driveway," I said. I knocked one more time, as hard as I could. To my surprise, the front door swung in a little.

"Hey—the door is open!" I called to Lily. She hurried back to the step. I pushed the door open a little further. "Anyone home?" I called in.

No reply.

"Hey—your door is open!" I shouted.

Lily pushed the door all the way, and we stepped inside. "Manny?" she called, cupping her hands around her mouth. "Manny?"

I stepped into the living room—and gasped.

I tried to speak. But I couldn't. I couldn't believe what I saw.

Lily grabbed my arm as we both stared around the living room.

The room was totally bare. No furniture. No curtains. No paintings or posters on the wall. Even the carpet had been removed, leaving shiny dark floorboards.

"Wh-where have they gone?" I managed to choke out.

Lily made her way through the black hall to the kitchen. Also empty. Everything gone. An empty hole where the refrigerator had stood.

"They've moved!" Lily exclaimed. "I don't believe it!"

"But why didn't Manny tell us?" I demanded, my eyes narrowing around the deserted room. "Why didn't he tell us his family was moving away?"

Lily shook her head and didn't reply. The house was silent. I could hear water dripping from the gutter outside.

"Maybe they had to move suddenly," Lily said finally.

"Suddenly? Why?" I demanded.

It was a question that neither of us could answer.

I love to run.

Not when I'm running from snarling dogs. But I do love to run.

I like the way it gets my heart pounding. And I like the *thud* of my trainers on the ground, and the feeling of my muscles all working together.

On Saturday mornings I like to go jogging with my dad. He always jogs at Miller Woods, along a path that curves around a small lake.

It's really pretty there. The air is always fresh-smelling. And it's a very quiet place.

Dad is tall and lean and pretty athletic. He used to be blond like me, but now his hair is mostly grey, and he has a big bald spot on top.

He jogs every morning before work. I think he usually jogs pretty fast. But on Saturdays, he slows down so that we can run side by side.

We usually jog without talking. That way he can concentrate on the scenery and the fresh air.

But this Saturday morning, I felt like talking. I had decided to tell Dad everything. About the bottle of INSTA-TAN. And about the black hair that kept sprouting.

73

As I talked, I kept my eyes straight ahead. I saw two big crows float down from the clear blue sky and perch side by side on the bare limb of a tree. The crows cawed loudly, as if talking to us.

The lake sparkled brightly as Dad and I followed the curving path around it. Small patches of ice bobbed in the blue-green water.

I started at the beginning and told the whole story. Dad slowed down a little more to listen. But we kept jogging as I talked.

I told him about finding the bottle of tanning lotion and how we all splashed it on ourselves as a joke. Dad nodded but kept his eyes straight ahead. "I guess it didn't work," he said, sounding a little breathless from running. "You don't look too tanned, Larry."

"No, it didn't work," I continued. "The bottle was really old, Dad. It had expired a long time ago."

I took a deep breath. The next part was the hardest to tell. "It didn't give me a tan, Dad. But something really weird started happening to me."

He kept jogging. We both leaped over a fallen tree branch. I slipped over a pile of wet leaves, but quickly caught my balance.

"This weird hair started growing on me," I told him in a shaky voice. "First on the back of my hand. Then on both hands. Then on my knees."

Dad stopped. He turned to me with a worried expression on his face. "Hair?"

I nodded, breathing hard. "Black hair. Thick clumps of it. Very rough and spiky."

Dad swallowed hard. His eyes grew wide. With surprise? With fear? With disbelief?

I couldn't tell.

But to my surprise, he grabbed my arm and started to pull me. "Come on, Larry. We've got to go."

"But, Dad—" I started, holding back.

He tightened his grip and pulled harder. "I *said* we've got to *go*!" he insisted through gritted teeth. "Now!"

He tugged so hard, he nearly pulled me off my feet!

"Dad—what's wrong?" I demanded in a high, shrill voice. "What is it?"

He didn't answer. He pulled me back along the path towards the street. His eyes were wild. His whole face was twisted into a tight, frightened scowl.

"Dad—what's wrong?" I cried. "Where are you taking me? Where?"

75

Dr Murkin raised the hypodermic needle and examined it in the light. "Turn away, Larry," he said softly. "I know you don't like to watch. This won't hurt at all."

Pain shot through my arm as the needle sank in. I shut my eyes and held my breath until he pulled out the needle.

"I know it's early," he said, rubbing my arm with a cotton wool ball dipped in alcohol. "But since you were here, I thought I'd give you your shot."

My dad sat tensely in a folding chair against the wall of the small examining room. He had his arms crossed tightly over the front of his sweatshirt.

"Wh-what about the hair?" I stammered to Dr Murkin. "Did the INSTA-TAN—"

The doctor shook his head. "I really don't think tanning lotion can cause hair to grow, Larry. Those lotions work on the pigments of the skin. They—"

"But it was a very old bottle!" I insisted. "Maybe the ingredients turned sour or something!"

He waved his hand, as if to say, "No way."

Then he turned and started scribbling notes in my file. "I'm sorry, Larry," he said, writing rapidly in a tiny handwriting. "It wasn't the tanning lotion. Trust me."

He turned his head to me, his eyes studying me. "I've examined you from head to foot. You passed every test. You seem fine to me."

"Whew! That's a relief!" Dad said, sighing.

"But the hair—!" I insisted.

"Let's wait and see," Dr Murkin replied, his eyes on my dad.

"Wait and see?" I cried. "You're not going to give me any medicine or anything to stop it?"

"Maybe it won't happen again," Dr Murkin said. He closed my file. Then he motioned for me to jump down from the examining table.

"Try not to worry, Larry," he said, handing my coat to me. "You'll be okay."

"Thank you, Dr Murkin," Dad said, climbing to his feet. He flashed the doctor a smile, but I could see that it was forced. Dad still looked really tense.

I followed Dad out to the car park. We didn't say anything until we were in the car and on the way home. "Feel better?" Dad asked, his eyes narrowed straight ahead on the road.

"No," I replied glumly.

"What's wrong?" Dad asked impatiently. "Dr Murkin said you checked out fine."

"What about the ugly black hair?" I demanded angrily. "What about it? Why didn't he do anything about it? Do you think he didn't believe me?"

"I'm sure he believed you," Dad said softly.

"Then why didn't he do anything to help me?" I wailed.

Dad didn't reply for the longest time. He stared straight through the windscreen, chewing his lower lip. Then, finally, he said in a hushed voice, "Sometimes the best thing is to wait."

We met at Lily's house for band practice that afternoon. We sounded pretty good—but it wasn't the same without Manny.

We were all really upset that he had moved away without saying goodbye. Lily asked her mum to call some friends who were friendly with Manny's parents. She wanted to find out where Manny and his family had moved.

But the friends turned out to be as surprised as we were.

We couldn't find anyone who knew that Manny's family planned to move from our town.

I have to admit that our songs sounded better with two guitars instead of three. Lily has a very light singing voice—not much power. And three guitars nearly always drowned her out.

With Manny gone, we could actually hear Lily some of the time.

I kept messing up the Beatles song we were rehearsing—"I Want to Hold Your Hand". I played the wrong chords and couldn't get the rhythm right.

I knew what the trouble was. I couldn't stop thinking about Dr Murkin and how he didn't believe me about the hair. He said it wasn't the INSTA-TAN. But maybe he was wrong.

I felt so angry—and so . . . alone.

Glancing around Lily's living room as we started "I Want to Hold Your Hand" for the twentieth time, I studied my friends. Were they having the same problem? Were they growing ugly, black hair, too, and afraid to tell anyone?

The first time I had asked, Lily had laughed at me and called me Hairy Larry. But I had to ask again. I couldn't think about anything else. I had to know the truth.

I waited till practice was over. Kristina was tucking her guitar into its case. Jared went into the kitchen to get a Coke from the fridge. Lily was standing beside the couch, one hand twirling the gold pirate coin at her throat.

"I—I have to ask you something," I said nervously when Jared returned to the room.

He popped the top of the can, and a spray of Coke hit him in the face.

Everyone laughed.

"Can't you work a Coke can?" Lily joked. "Do you need an instruction book?"

"Ha-ha," Jared replied sarcastically, wiping his face with his sleeve. "You deliberately shook the cans, Lily, so people would get squirted. Admit it."

Kristina laughed as she snapped her guitar case shut. "Maybe you should stick to juice cartons, Jared."

He stuck out his tongue at her.

I cleared my throat loudly. "I want to ask you guys something," I repeated in a shaky voice.

They were all in a great mood, laughing and kidding around. They all seemed totally normal.

Why was I the only one who felt worried and afraid?

"Remember the INSTA-TAN stuff?" I started. "Have any of you been growing hair since we put that stuff on?" I could feel my face turning red. "I mean, really ugly patches of black hair?"

Jared started to laugh, and Coke spurted out of his nose. He started to choke. Kristina hurried over to slap him on the back.

"Hairy Larry!" Jared cried when he stopped choking. He pointed the Coke can at me and started chanting. "Hairy Larry! Hairy Larry!"

"Come on, guys!" I pleaded. "I'm serious!"

That made Kristina and Jared laugh even harder.

I turned to Lily, who was still standing beside the couch. She had a troubled expression on her face. She definitely wasn't laughing. She lowered her eyes to the floor as I continued to stare at her.

"Larry is a werewolf!" Jared declared.

"I hope The Geeks don't have to play when there's a full moon!" Kristina exclaimed.

"Maybe Larry's howling is better than his guitar playing!" Jared said. They both laughed.

"I—I was just making a joke!" I stammered. I wanted a hole to open up in the floor so that I could disappear into it.

I'm the only one, I realized. *I'm the only one who is growing the ugly hair.*

That's why Jared and Kristina thought it was so funny. It wasn't happening to them. They didn't have to worry about it.

But Lily wasn't joining in with the jokes. She turned away and started picking up music sheets from the floor and straightening the room.

Lily always enjoys teasing me and making me blush. I stared at her, wondering if she had the same secret I did.

I packed up my guitar slowly and waited for Jared and Kristina to leave. Then I put on my

81

coat and baseball cap and followed Lily to the front door.

On the front step, I turned back to her. "Lily, tell me the truth," I insisted, studying her face. "Have you been growing weird patches of black hair on your hands and knees?"

She hesitated, chewing her bottom lip. "I . . . I don't want to talk about it," she replied in a whisper.

Then she slammed the front door.

I didn't move from the concrete step. I kept picturing her troubled expression. I kept hearing her whispered voice.

Was it happening to Lily? If it was, why wouldn't she admit it to me? Was she too embarrassed?

Or was she embarrassed for *me*?

Maybe it wasn't happening to her, I realized. Maybe she just thinks I'm crazy. Maybe she feels bad for me because I keep acting like such a jerk.

Feeling totally confused, I turned and headed for the street. The sun was still high in the sky, but the air felt cold. A sharp wind blew at my face as I started towards home.

Leaning into the wind, I reached up and tugged down my cap to keep it from blowing away. To my surprise, I couldn't pull it down.

The cap suddenly felt tight. Too tight.

I removed it and held it close to my feet to

study it. Had someone adjusted the back to make it tighter?

No.

A chill of dread ran down my back as I raised a hand to my forehead. And discovered why my cap didn't fit.

My entire forehead was covered with thick, bristly hair.

I burst through the back door, into the kitchen. "Mum—look at this!" I cried. "Look at my head!"

My eyes darted around the room. "Mum?"

Not there.

I ran through the house, calling for her. I decided it was time to show my parents what was happening to me. Time to make them believe me.

The stripe of hair would totally gross them out, would finally convince them this was *serious*.

"Mum? Dad? Anybody home?"

No.

When I returned to the kitchen, I found a note on the refrigerator: *WE WENT SHOPPING IN BROOKESDALE VILLAGE. HOME LATE. FIX YOURSELF A SNACK.*

With a cry of disgust, I tossed my cap across the room. Then I pulled off my parka and let it fall to the floor.

My heart pounding, I made my way to the mirror in the front hall and studied myself. I looked like some kind of comic book mutant!

My pale face stared back at me. It appeared exactly the same. Except that I had a thick, black stripe of fur across my forehead.

Looks like I'm wearing a bandanna, I thought miserably. Like one of those headbands that skiers wear. Except this one is made of disgusting hair.

I ran a trembling hand over the thick hair.

My chest heaved up and down. I felt like crying and screaming furiously at the same time. I felt like grabbing the stripe of fur and ripping it out of my head.

I couldn't bear to look at myself. The hair was so gross, so disgusting.

I decided there was no way I could wait for Mum and Dad to get home. I couldn't leave that horrible hair on my face. Spinning away from the mirror, I ran upstairs to shave it off.

I lathered up the strip of hair with shaving cream. Then I began to scrape my dad's razor over it.

"Ow!" It hurt, but I didn't care. I had to cut it off. Every thick, bristly strand of it.

Watching the hair fall into the sink, I suddenly knew what I had to do. I had to find the INSTA-TAN bottle. I had to find it and take it to Dr Murkin.

If I bring him the bottle, I can make him believe me! I told myself. Then Dr Murkin can do tests on it. He can figure out why it's making hair grow on me.

And once he knows that it's the INSTA-TAN that's growing hair, Dr Murkin will give me a cure, I decided.

But where did we throw the bottle?

I shut my eyes and struggled to remember.

After I discovered the bottle, we had all run into Lily's house to splash the stuff on. Then we had gone back outside to mess around in the snow.

Did we throw the INSTA-TAN bottle back in the bin next door?

I had to find out.

I scribbled a note to my parents, telling them I'd left something at Lily's and would be back soon. Then I grabbed my coat and hurried out of the door.

The air had become a lot colder. Clouds had rolled over the sun, making the evening sky grey. I zipped up my parka and pulled the hood over my head. My forehead still tingled from where I had shaved it.

The three blocks to Lily's house seemed like three miles! As I turned the corner, her house came into view.

I don't want her to see me, I realized. If she sees me poking around that bin, she'll want to know why. And I'm not ready to tell her the whole story.

She wouldn't tell *me* the truth, I thought bitterly. Instead, she slammed the door on me.

So I'm not ready to tell her the truth, either.

I felt glad that it had become so dark out. Maybe Lily wouldn't see me.

I kept my eyes on her house as I approached. The lights were on in the dining room. Maybe her family was having an early dinner.

Good, I thought. I'll dig into the bin, pull out the bottle, and disappear before they finish, before anyone has a chance to glance out of the window.

I stopped short when I saw that there was just one little problem.

The bin was gone.

The workers must have hauled it away.

I let out a long sigh and nearly slumped to my knees. "Now what?" I murmured out loud.

Now how do I prove to Dr Murkin that the INSTA-TAN is making me grow hair?

The cold wind swirled around me as I stared at the kerb where the bin had stood. Fat brown leaves, blown by the twisting wind, fluttered around my legs.

I shivered.

Turning to leave, a memory flashed through my mind.

The INSTA-TAN bottle. We *hadn't* dropped it

back into the bin. We had thrown it into the woods on the other side of the neighbours' house.

"Yes!" I cried happily. "Yes!"

We had chased each other across the neighbours' garden—and I'd heaved the bottle into the trees.

It will still be there, I told myself. It *has* to be there.

I darted past Lily's house, glancing up at the front windows. I couldn't see anyone looking out.

Past the neighbours' house, dark and empty. The rebuilding work not finished.

Into the woods. The dead leaves wet and slippery under my shoes. The bare tree branches shook and rattled in the shifting, sharp wind.

Where had the bottle landed? I asked myself. Where?

It hadn't gone far, I remembered. Just past the first trees.

It had to be nearby, I knew. Somewhere near where I stood.

A blanket of deep shadow had fallen over the woods. I kicked at a pile of dead leaves. My shoe hit something hard.

Bending quickly, I scooped leaves away with both hands.

Only a tree branch.

I moved deeper into the woods, pushing my way through clumps of tall, dead weeds.

I stopped.

It had to be around here, I knew. My eyes desperately searched the shadows.

There it is. No. Just a smooth stone.

I kicked it away. Then I turned slowly, making a complete circle, my eyes sweeping the dark ground.

Where is the bottle? Where?

I sucked in my breath when I heard the sound.

The crack of a twig.

I listened hard. I heard the crackle of leaves. The brush of a leg against a winter-dry shrub.

Another twig cracking.

Swallowing hard, I realized I was no longer alone.

"Wh-who's there?" I called.

"Who's there?"

No reply.

Frozen as still as a statue, I listened. I heard the scrape of feet moving rapidly over the ground. I heard heavy breathing.

"Hey—who is it?" I called.

I glanced down—and saw the bottle. Lying on its side, nestled in a pile of leaves right in front of me.

I bent quickly, reached eagerly for the bottle with both hands. But I jerked back up to my feet in fright as a dark figure lumbered out from the trees.

Panting hard. Its long tongue flapping from its open mouth.

A tall, brown dog. Even in the dim light, I could see how scraggly and tangled its fur was. I could see large burrs stuck in its heaving side.

I took a step back. "Are you alone, boy?" I

called in a frightened whisper. "Huh? Are you alone, doggie?"

The animal lowered its head and let out a whimper.

I searched the woods for other dogs. Was he part of a pack? Part of the pack of stray dogs that liked to chase me, growling and snapping?

I couldn't see any others.

"Good dog," I told him, keeping my voice low and calm. "Good doggie."

He stared up at me, still panting. His scraggly, brown tail wagged once, then drooped.

I bent slowly, keeping my eyes on the dog, and picked up the bottle. It felt surprisingly cold. I held it up and tried to see if any of the liquid remained inside.

But it was too dark to see.

I'm pretty sure I didn't use every last drop, I thought, struggling to remember. There has to be a little left. Enough for Dr Murkin to test.

I shook the bottle close to my ear, listening for the splash of liquid inside. *Please, please, let there be a drop left!* I pleaded silently.

The trees shivered in a sharp, swirling gust. Leaves rustled and scraped against each other.

The dog let out another soft whimper.

I grasped the bottle tightly in my right hand and started to back away. "Bye-bye, doggie."

He tilted his head and stared up at me.

I took another step back. "Bye, doggie," I repeated softly. "Go home. Go home, boy."

He didn't move. He let out another whimper. Then his tail began to wag.

I took another step back, grasping the INSTA-TAN bottle tightly. Then, as I started to turn away from the staring dog, I saw the others.

They poked out quickly, silently, from the dark trees. Five or six big dogs, their eyes glowing angrily. Then five or six more.

As they lumbered nearer, moving quickly, steadily, I could hear their growls, low and menacing. They pulled back their lips and bared their teeth.

I froze, staring in terror at their darkly glowing eyes, listening to their menacing, low growls.

Then I spun around awkwardly. Started to run.

"Ohh!" I let out a shrill cry as I stumbled over a fallen tree branch.

The bottle flew out of my hand.

As I fell, I reached out for it, grasping desperately.

Missed.

I watched in horror as it hit a sharp rock— and shattered. The jagged pieces flew in all directions. A tiny puddle of brown liquid washed over the rock.

I landed hard on my knees and elbows. Pain shot through my body. But I ignored it and scrambled to my feet.

I whirled around to face the dogs.

But to my surprise, they were running in a different direction. Through the trees, I glimpsed a frightened rabbit, scrabbling over the leafy ground. Barking and growling, the dogs chased after it.

My heart pounding, my knees still throbbing, I walked over to the rock and stared down at the jagged pieces of orange glass. I picked one up and examined it closely.

"*Now* what do I do?" I asked myself out loud. I could still hear the excited barking of the dogs in the distance. "Now what?"

The bottle was shattered into a dozen pieces. My evidence was gone. I had nothing to show Dr Murkin. Nothing at all.

With an angry cry, I tossed the piece of glass at the trees. Then I wearily slunk towards home.

Mum and Dad hurried to a school meeting after dinner. I went upstairs to my room to do my homework.

I didn't feel like being alone.

I took Jasper in my lap and petted her for a while. But she wasn't in the mood. She glared at me with those weird yellow eyes. When that didn't work, she scratched my hand, jumped away, and disappeared out of the room.

I tried calling Lily, but no one answered at her place.

Outside, the wind howled around the corner of the house. It made my bedroom windows rattle.

A chill ran down my back.

I leaned my elbows on my desk and hunched over my government textbook. But I couldn't concentrate. The words on the page became a grey blur.

I walked across the room and picked up my guitar. Then I bent down and plugged it into my amp.

Lots of times when I'm feeling nervous or upset, I play my guitar for a while. It always calms me down.

I cranked the amp up really high and started to play a loud blues melody. There was no one else in, no one to tell me to turn it down. I wanted to play as loud as I could—loud enough to drown out my troubled thoughts.

But I had played for only three or four minutes when I realized that something was wrong.

I kept missing notes. Messing up the chords.

What's wrong with me? I wondered. I've played this tune a million times. I can play it in my sleep.

When I glanced down at my fingers, I saw the problem.

"Ohh!" I uttered a weak groan. That disgusting hair had sprouted over both of my hands. My fingers were covered in thick, black hair.

I turned my hands over. Both palms were covered, too.

The guitar fell heavily to the floor as I jumped to my feet.

My arms began to itch.

With trembling hands, I tore at the cuffs. Pulled up the sleeves.

My arms were covered, too! The thick, bristly hair swept over both arms and hands.

I stood there, swallowing hard, staring down at my hairy arms and hands. My legs were trembling. I felt weak.

My mouth suddenly felt dry. My throat ached. I tried to swallow.

Was the disgusting hair growing on my *tongue*?

Feeling a jolt of nausea, I lurched across the hall to the bathroom. Clicking on the ceiling light, I leaned over the sink. I brought my face up close to the mirror and stuck out my tongue.

No.

My tongue was okay.

But my face—my cheeks and chin—were covered with black hair.

It's spreading so fast! I realized. The mirror reflected my horror.

It's spreading so fast now—all over me.
What am I going to do?
Isn't there *anything* I can do?

96

I got to school early on Monday morning and waited for Lily at her locker.

It had taken hours to shave off all the bristly clumps of hair. But I'd done it.

This morning I wore a sweater with extra-long sleeves, and I pulled a baseball cap down low on my head in case the hair grew back during the day.

"Lily, where are you?" I murmured impatiently. I paced nervously back and forth in front of the row of green lockers.

Lily and I have to face this problem together, I told myself. I remembered the frightened expression on Lily's face when I asked her if she had been growing weird hair.

I *knew* the same thing was happening to Lily. I just knew it.

And I knew that Lily must be embarrassed like me, too embarrassed to admit it, to talk about it.

But the two of us can work out what to do, I decided.

If the two of us go to Dr Murkin and tell him about the INSTA-TAN lotion and the hair, he'll *have* to believe us.

But where was Lily?

Kids jammed the hall, slamming lockers, laughing and talking. I glanced at my watch. Only three minutes till the bell rang.

"How's it going, Larry?" a voice called.

I turned and saw Howie Hurwin grinning at me. His sister, Marissa, stood beside him. Her plait was caught in her backpack strap, and she was struggling to free it.

"Hi, Howie," I said, sighing. He was the *last* person I wanted to see this morning!

"Ready for tomorrow?" he asked. Why did he have to grin like that when he talked? That grin just made me want to punch him.

"Tomorrow?" I glanced down the crowded hall, searching for Lily.

Howie laughed. "Have you forgotten about the Battle of the Bands?"

"Ow!" Marissa cried. She finally managed to tug her plait free. "Is your band still going to play?" she asked. "We heard about Manny leaving."

"Yeah. We'll be there," I told her. "We sound pretty good."

"We do, too!" Howie replied, grinning even

wider. "We might be on TV. My uncle knows a woman who works on *Star Search*. He thinks maybe he can get us on."

"Great," I replied, without any enthusiasm. Where was Lily?

"If we get on that show, we'll probably win," Marissa added, still fiddling with her long plait. "And then we'll be famous."

"They've asked us to play at the next school dance," Howie said. "They haven't asked *your* band, have they?"

"No," I replied. "No one's asked us."

That made Howie's grin practically burst off his face. "Too bad," he said.

The bell rang. "I've got to go," I said, hurrying towards Miss Shindling's room.

"See you at the contest tomorrow," Marissa called.

"We're going first," Howie shouted. "I guess they're saving the best for *first*!"

I heard the two of them laughing as I stepped into the classroom. I made my way to my seat, searching for Lily. Had she slipped past me while I was talking with Howie and Marissa?

No. No sign of her.

I sank into my seat, feeling worried and disappointed. Was Lily sick today? I hoped not. She can't get sick the day before the Battle of the Bands, I told myself. She just can't.

"Larry, would you hand out the tests?" Miss

Shindling asked, dropping a heavy stack of papers into my arms.

"Huh? Test?"

I had totally forgotten.

Lily didn't come to school. I tried phoning her at lunchtime. The phone rang and rang, but no one answered.

After school, I decided to go to Lily's house to see what had happened to her. But as I walked out of the school building, I remembered that my mum had asked me to come straight home after school. She had some chores she wanted me to help her with.

It was a clear, cold day. Puffy, white clouds floated high in the afternoon sky. All the snow had finally melted, but the ground was still soft and wet.

I waited for several cars to pass. Then I crossed the street and headed for home.

I had walked nearly a block when I realized I was being followed.

A dog brushed softly against my leg. Startled, I stopped and stared down at it.

The dog had light brown fur, almost red, with a white patch at its throat. It was a medium-sized dog, a little bigger than a cocker spaniel. It had long, floppy brown ears and a long, furry tail that swept slowly back and forth as it gazed up at me.

"Who are you?" I asked it. "I've never seen *you* before."

I glanced around, making sure there weren't a dozen other dogs lurking in the bushes, getting ready to chase after me.

Then I turned and started walking again.

The dog brushed my leg again and kept on going. As I walked, it stayed a few metres ahead of me, glancing back to make sure I was following.

"Are you following *me*—or am I following *you*?" I called to it.

The dog's tail gave a single wag in reply.

It followed me all the way home.

My mum was waiting for me in the driveway. She had a long green sweater pulled down over her jeans. "Nice day," she commented, glancing up at the sunny sky.

"Hi, Mum," I greeted her. "This dog followed me home."

The dog sniffed at the low evergreen shrubs that lined the front walk.

"She's rather pretty," Mum said. "What a nice colour. Who does she belong to?"

I shrugged. "Beats me. I've never seen her before."

The dog came over and stared up at Mum.

"At least she's friendly," I said, setting my heavy backpack down on the driveway. "Maybe we should keep her."

"No way," Mum replied sharply. "No dogs. Not with Jasper in the house."

I bent down and petted the top of the dog's head.

"She has a tag on her collar," Mum said, pointing. "Check it out, Larry. Maybe it says the owner's name."

The dog's tail wagged furiously as I petted her head. "Good dog," I said softly.

"Come on, Larry. See what the tag says," Mum insisted.

"Okay, okay." I reached for the round, gold tag hanging down from the dog's collar. Then I dropped to my knees and lowered my face so that I could see it clearly.

"Huh?"

I recognized it instantly.

It wasn't a dog tag. It was Lily's gold pirate coin.

I nearly fell over. I felt as if someone had kicked me in the stomach.

"M-mum!" I stammered. But my voice came out as a gasp.

"Larry—what are you doing?" Mum called. She had wandered to the side of the driveway and was pulling up some dead weeds. "What does the tag say?"

"It—it isn't a tag," I finally managed to choke out.

She turned her head back to me. "Huh?"

"It isn't a dog tag," I repeated, still holding it between my fingers. "It's Lily's gold pirate coin."

Mum laughed. "Why would Lily give her coin to a dog? Didn't her grandfather give her that coin?"

"I—I don't know why," I stammered. "I don't get it, Mum."

The dog's hot breath brushed over my hand.

103

She pulled away from me, settled back, and started scratching her long, floppy ear with her back paw.

"Are you sure it's a gold coin, Larry?" Mum asked, crossing the drive, standing right behind me.

I nodded and reached for the coin again. "Yeah. It's Lily's gold coin, Mum."

"It must be some *other* gold coin," Mum suggested. "I'm sure it isn't the same coin."

Mum must be right, I decided.

I let go of the coin and raised my hand to pet the dog's head.

But my hand stopped in mid-air when I saw the dog's eyes.

She had one blue eye and one green eye.

"It's Lily! It's Lily!" I shrieked, jumping to my feet.

My shouts frightened the dog. She uttered a shrill *yip*, turned, and bolted from the front garden.

"Lily—come back!" I called after her. "Come back! Lily!"

"Larry—wait!" Mum cried. "Please—!"

I didn't hear the rest of what she said. Jumping over my backpack, I darted towards the street. I hurtled across without slowing to look for cars—and kept running towards Lily's house.

It *is* Lily! I told myself. That dog has a green eye and a blue eye. And it's wearing Lily's coin!

It *is* Lily! I *know* it!

I could hear my mum calling for me to come back. But I ignored her and kept running.

Lily's house was three blocks away. I ran at full speed the whole way. By the time her house came into view, I was gasping for breath, and I had a sharp pain in my side.

But I didn't care.

I had to see Lily. I had to know for sure that the dog wasn't Lily.

Such a crazy thought! As I crossed the street, I started to realize how crazy it was.

Lily, a dog?

Larry, are you totally losing it? I asked myself. Mum must think I'm totally wacko! I realized.

Lily, a dog?

I slowed down, rubbing the pain at my side, trying to massage it away.

I spotted Lily's parents in the driveway. The boot of their blue Chevy was open. Mr Vonn was lifting a suitcase into it.

"Hi!" I called breathlessly. "Hey—hi!"

"Hello, Larry," Mrs Vonn said as I stepped up to the car. I saw two other suitcases and some smaller bags waiting to be loaded into the car.

"Going on a trip?" I asked, struggling to catch my breath. The pain in my side kept throbbing, refusing to go away.

They didn't answer. Mr Vonn groaned as he hoisted a heavy suitcase into the boot.

"Where's Lily?" I asked. I handed him one of the smaller bags. "She wasn't in school today."

"We're going away," Mrs Vonn said quietly from behind me.

"Well, where's Lily?" I repeated. "Is she inside?"

Mr Vonn frowned, but didn't reply.

I turned to Lily's mum. "Can I see her?" I asked impatiently. "Is Lily inside?"

"You must have the wrong house," she replied softly.

My mouth dropped open. "Wrong house? Mrs Vonn—what do you mean?"

"There's no one here named Lily," she said.

For some reason, I burst out laughing.

Startled laughter. Frightened laughter.

Mrs Vonn's sad expression cut my laughter short—and sent a chill down my back.

"Is Lily—?" I started to say.

Mrs Vonn grabbed my shoulder and squeezed it. She lowered her face close to mine. "Listen to what I'm telling you, Larry," she said through gritted teeth.

"But—but—" I sputtered.

"There *is* no Lily," she repeated, squeezing my shoulder hard. "Just forget about her." She had tears in her eyes.

Mr Vonn slammed the car boot. I jumped out of Mrs Vonn's grasp, my heart pounding.

"You'd better go," Mr Vonn said firmly, coming over to join his wife.

I took a step back. My legs felt weak and shaky.

"But, Lily—" I started.

"You'd better go," Mr Vonn repeated.

At the side of the garage, I spotted the red-brown dog. She whimpered sadly, her head hung low.

I whirled round and ran, as fast as I could.

Mum and Dad acted so strange at dinner. They refused to discuss Lily or the dog or Lily's parents.

Mum and Dad kept glancing at each other, giving each other meaningful looks that I wasn't supposed to see.

They think I'm crazy! I realized. That's why they're refusing to talk about it. They think I'm losing my mind. They don't want to say anything to me until they decide how they're going to handle me.

"I'm not crazy!" I shouted suddenly, dropping my fork and knife on to the table. I hadn't touched my spaghetti and meatballs.

How could I eat?

"I'm not crazy! I'm not making this up!"

"Can't we talk about it another time?" Mum pleaded, glancing at Dad.

"Let's just finish our dinner," Dad added, keeping his eyes on his plate.

After dinner, I called Jared and Kristina over to give them the bad news. I didn't want them to think that I was crazy. So I simply told them that Lily had gone away.

"But what about tomorrow?" Jared cried.

"Yeah. What about the Battle of the Bands?" Kristina demanded. "How could Lily leave on the day before the contest?"

I shrugged. We were sitting in the living room. Kristina and I sat on opposite ends of the couch. Jared was sprawled in the chair across from me.

Jasper brushed over my feet. I leaned down and lifted her into my lap. Her yellow eyes stared up at me. Then she closed them and settled against me, purring softly.

"Where did Lily go?" Kristina asked angrily, drumming her fingers on the couch arm. "On holiday? Why didn't she tell us she was going to miss the contest?"

"Howie Hurwin will jump for joy when he hears this news," Jared muttered glumly, shaking his head.

"I don't know where Lily went," I told them. "I saw her parents loading suitcases into the car. Now they're gone. That's all I know. I'm sure Lily is very unhappy. I know Lily wanted to be with us. I don't think she had a choice."

I had a sudden urge to tell them everything that had happened. But I didn't want them to start laughing at me. Or worrying about me.

I felt so mixed up. I didn't know what I wanted to do.

I wanted Lily back. And Manny. That I knew.

And I wanted the ugly hair to stop sprouting all over my body.

If only I had never found that bottle of INSTA-TAN.

This was all my fault. All of it.

"So I suppose The Geeks have to pull out of the band contest tomorrow," I said glumly.

"I suppose so," Jared repeated, shaking his head.

"No way!" Kristina cried, surprising both of us. She jumped to her feet and stood between Jared and me. She balled both hands into fists. "No way!" she repeated.

"But we don't have a singer—" Jared protested.

"I can sing," Kristina replied quickly. "I'm a pretty good singer."

"But you haven't rehearsed any of the songs," Jared said. "Do you know the words?"

Kristina nodded. "All of them."

"But, Kristina—" I started.

"Listen, guys," she said sharply, "we *have* to go on stage tomorrow. Even if it's just the three of us. We can't let Howie Hurwin win tomorrow—can we?"

"I'd like to wipe that grin off Howie's face," I muttered.

"Me, too," Jared agreed. "But how can we? Two guitars and a keyboard? Howie has his full band. He'll blast us out of the auditorium."

"Not if we play our hearts out!" Kristina exclaimed with emotion. "Not if we give it our best."

"Let's do it for Lily!" I blurted out. The words just tumbled from my mouth. As soon as I said it, I felt embarrassed.

But Kristina and Jared picked right up on it. "Let's do it for Lily!" they both cried. "We can win! We really can! Let's win it for Lily!"

So it was decided. The Geeks would go on stage tomorrow afternoon. Could we win? Could we beat Howie and the Shouters?

Probably not.

But we'd give it our best shot.

"Let's go up to my room and practise a little," I suggested.

Jared started towards the stairs. But Kristina didn't move.

I turned and found her staring at my face in horror.

"Larry—!" she cried, pointing. "What's *that* on your forehead?"

112

I gasped in horror.

My hand shot up to my forehead.

The ugly black hair—it had grown back, I knew. And now Kristina and Jared were both staring at it. They both saw it—saw that I was becoming some kind of hairy monster.

I rubbed my forehead with a trembling hand.

Smooth.

My forehead was smooth!

"It's right there." Kristina pointed.

I hurried over to the hallway mirror and gazed up at my forehead. I discovered an orange smear near my right temple.

"It's spaghetti sauce," I moaned. "I must have rubbed my face during dinner."

I rubbed off the orange spot. My entire body was shaking. Kristina had scared me to death! Over a stupid spot of spaghetti sauce!

"Larry, are you okay?" she asked, standing

behind me and staring at my reflection in the mirror. "You look a bit weird."

"I'm okay," I replied quickly, trying to force my body to stop shaking and quaking.

"Hey—don't get sick," Jared warned. "Kristina and I can't go on the stage by ourselves tomorrow."

"I'll be there," I told them. "Don't worry, guys. I'll be there."

The next afternoon, the whole school jammed into the auditorium to watch the Battle of the Bands.

Feeling really nervous, I stood backstage and peeked out through the curtain. The lights in the auditorium were all on, and Mr Fosburg, the principal, stood in front of the curtain, both arms raised, trying to get everyone quiet.

Behind me, Howie Hurwin and his band were tuning up, adjusting the amps, making sure the sound was right. Marissa was wearing a very short, sparkly red dress over black tights. She caught me staring at her and flashed me a smug smile.

The Geeks should have dressed up, I realized, watching Marissa. We didn't even think of it. The three of us were wearing T-shirts and jeans, our normal school clothes.

I turned and gazed at Howie's new synthesizer keyboard. It was about a mile long, and it had a thousand buttons and dials on it. It made Jared's keyboard look like a baby toy.

Howie caught me staring at it. "Cool, huh?" he called, grinning that gruesome grin of his. "Hey, Larry—after we win the contest, you can have my autograph!"

Howie laughed. So did Marissa and the rest of the Shouters.

I turned and slumped away to join Jared and Kristina at the side of the stage. "We're total losers," I moaned, shaking my head.

"Good attitude, Larry," Jared replied sarcastically.

"Maybe Howie's giant keyboard will blow out all the fuses," I said glumly. "That's our only chance."

Kristina rolled her eyes. "They can't be *that* good," she muttered.

But they were.

The auditorium lights darkened. The curtain slid open. Howie and the Shouters stepped into the red-and-blue stage lights. And began blasting out the old Chuck Berry rock-and-roll song "Johnny B. Goode".

They sounded great. And they looked great.

Marissa's dress sparkled in the light. They had worked out dance moves, and they all danced and moved as they played.

We should have thought of that, I told myself glumly, watching from the side of the stage.

115

When *we* play, the three of us just stand around—like *geeks*!

The kids in the auditorium went crazy. They all jumped to their feet and began clapping along, moving and dancing.

They stayed on their feet for all four of the Shouters' songs. Each song came louder and faster than the last. The old auditorium rocked and shook so hard, I thought the floor might cave in!

Then, as Howie and Marissa and the others took their bows, the auditorium erupted in wild cheers and shouts of, "More! Moooore! Mooooore!"

So Howie and the Shouters did two more songs.

Jared, Kristina and I kept casting tense glances at each other as they played. This wasn't doing a whole lot for our confidence!

Finally, Howie and Marissa took several more bows and ran off the stage, waving their fists high above their heads in triumph.

"Your turn!" Howie called to me as he ran past. He grinned. "Hey, Larry—where's the rest of your band?"

I started to reply angrily. But Jared gave me a hard shove, and the three of us moved uncertainly on to the stage.

I bent down and plugged my guitar into the amp. Jared worked quickly to adjust the sound level of his little keyboard.

Howie's giant keyboard had been pushed to the back of the stage. It seemed to stare at us, reminding us how good—and loud—the Shouters had sounded.

Kristina stood tensely at the microphone, her arms crossed in front of her T-shirt. I played a few chords, testing the level of the amp. My hands felt cold and sweaty. They slipped over the strings.

The audience was talking and laughing, restless, waiting for us to start.

"Are we ready?" I whispered to Jared and Kristina. "Let's do 'I Want to Hold Your Hand' first. Then go into the Rolling Stones song."

They nodded.

I took a deep breath and steadied my hands on my guitar.

Jared leaned over the keyboard. Kristina uncrossed her arms and stepped to the microphone, jamming both hands into her jeans pockets.

We started the Beatles song.

Shaky at first. All three of us sang on this one. And the harmony was off.

My guitar was too loud. It was drowning out our voices. I wanted to stop and turn it down. But of course I couldn't.

The audience sat quietly, listening. They didn't jump to their feet and start dancing.

They applauded loudly as we finished the

117

song. But it was polite applause. No loud cheering. No real enthusiasm.

At least we got through it! I told myself, wiping my sweaty hands on my jeans legs.

I stepped forward as we started the Rolling Stones song.

I had a really long guitar solo in this number. I was praying I didn't mess up.

I nodded to Jared and Kristina. Kristina grabbed the floor microphone with both hands, leaning close to it. Jared started the song on the keyboard.

I started my solo. Badly. I messed up the first chords.

My heart started to thump. My mouth was suddenly too dry to swallow.

I closed my eyes and tried to shut out everything—to concentrate on my fingers, on the music.

As I played, the audience started to cheer. A few shouts at first. Some scattered applause.

But then the cheering grew louder and louder.

Happily, I opened my eyes. Several kids were on their feet, shouting and laughing.

I bent my knees and let my fingers move over the frets, the pick moving automatically now over the strings.

I was starting to feel good—really good.

The cheers grew louder. I realized that several kids were pointing at me.

What's going on? I wondered.

And I suddenly knew that something was wrong. The cheers were *too* loud. The laughter was too loud. Too many kids were jumping up and pointing fingers at me.

"Great special effects!" I heard a boy shout from the first row.

"Yeah. Great special effects!"

Huh? I thought. *What* special effects?

It didn't take me long to work it out.

As Kristina started to sing, I reached my hand up and rubbed it over my face.

I cried out in horror as I felt the stiff, prickly hair.

My face was covered in it. My chin, my cheeks, my forehead.

The thick, black hair had sprouted over my entire face.

And the whole school was staring at it, staring at me.

The whole school knew my horrible, embarrassing secret.

25

"We won! We won!"

I heard Jared and Kristina shouting gleefully behind me.

But I set my guitar on the stage floor, turned away from them, and started to run.

The kids in the auditorium were still shouting and cheering.

We had won the contest because of my amazing hairy transformation. "Great special effects!" that kid had shouted. The "special effects" had won the day.

But I wasn't feeling like a winner.

I felt like an ugly freak.

The bushy hair had covered my face, then spread down to my neck and shoulders. Both hands were covered in bristly fur, and I could feel it growing up my arms. My back began to itch. Was it growing on my back, too?

"Hey, Larry—Larry!" I heard Kristina and Jared calling. "The trophy! Come and get your trophy!"

But I was out of the stage door, the wild cheers of the audience ringing in my ears. Out of the back door of the school. Into a chilly, grey afternoon. Dark clouds low over the trees.

Running now. Running blindly, my heart thudding.

Running home. Covered in thick, black fur.

Running in panic, in shame. In fear.

The houses and trees passed in a grey blur. As I turned up my driveway, I saw Mum and Dad back by the garage. They both turned to me, surprise on their faces.

"Look at me!" I shrieked. "Look!" My voice burst out, hoarse and terrified. "Now do you believe me?"

They gaped at me, their mouths wide open in shock and horror.

I held my hands up so they could see my arms. "Do you see my face?" I wailed. "See my arms? My hands?"

They both gasped. Mum grabbed Dad's arm.

"Now do you believe me?" I cried. "Now do you believe that the INSTA-TAN lotion makes hair grow?"

I stood staring at them, my chest heaving, panting loudly, tears in my eyes. I stood waiting, waiting for them to say something.

Finally, Mum broke the silence. "Larry, it isn't the tanning lotion," she said softly, holding tightly on to Dad. "We tried to keep it from you. But we can't any longer."

"Huh? Keep *what* from me?" I demanded.

They exchanged glances. Mum let out a sob. Dad slipped his arm around her.

"It isn't the tanning lotion," Dad said in a trembling voice. "Larry, you have to know the truth now. You're growing all that hair because you're not a human. You're a dog."

I bent down and lapped up some water from the plastic water bowl Mum and Dad put on the front step for me. It's so hard to drink without splashing water all over my snout.

Then I bounded down the steps on all fours and joined Lily over by the evergreen shrubs. We sniffed the shrubs for a while. Then we loped off to the next garden to see if there was anything interesting to sniff.

It's been two weeks since my human body vanished and I turned back into my real dog identity. Luckily, before I changed back, Mum and Dad—or, I should say, Mr and Mrs Boyd— were nice enough to explain to me what had happened.

They work for Dr Murkin, you see. In fact, everyone in the town works for Dr Murkin. The whole town is kind of an experimental testing lab.

A few years ago, Dr Murkin found a way to

change dogs into children. He discovered a serum that made us dogs look and think and act like people. That's what my shots were. He gave me fresh serum every two weeks.

But after a while, the serum doesn't work any more. It wears off. And the children go back to being dogs.

"Dr Murkin has decided to stop testing the serum on dogs," Mum told me. "It just doesn't work. And it causes the families too much pain when the children turn back into dogs."

"He's never going to work with dogs again," Dad explained. "The serum just doesn't last long enough with dogs. So, no more dogs."

It was nice of the Boyds to explain to me what had happened. I felt so grateful, I licked their hands. Then I ran off to find Lily and show her that I was a dog, too.

Lily and I roam around together all the time. Sometimes Manny joins us. There are so many dogs roaming around in this town. I guess they all were human for a while.

I'm glad Dr Murkin isn't using dogs for his tests any more. Dogs should be dogs, in my humble opinion.

Lily and I found some good dirt to sniff in the neighbours' flower garden. There aren't any flowers to dig up yet. But the dirt smells really great.

Then I saw the Boyds' car roll up the driveway.

They'd been gone all afternoon. I went running up eagerly to the car, wagging my tail happily.

I jumped up and barked out a greeting.

To my surprise, Mrs Boyd was carrying a baby. A tiny baby, tightly wrapped in pink blankets.

She held the baby in both arms, and carried it carefully up the walk towards the house. Mr Boyd had a big smile on his face as he caught up with her.

"What a good little girl," Mrs Boyd cooed to the baby. "Yes, you are. You're a good little girl. Welcome to your new home, Jasper."

Huh? I thought. Isn't Jasper a funny name for a little girl?

Then I stared up at the baby and saw her bright yellow eyes.

A Night in Terror Tower

"I'm scared," Eddie said.

I shivered and zipped my coat up to my chin. "Eddie, this was *your* idea," I told my brother. "I didn't beg and plead to see the Terror Tower. You did."

He raised his brown eyes to the tower. A strong gust of wind fluttered his dark brown hair. "I have a strange feeling about it, Sue. A bad feeling."

I made a disgusted face. "Eddie, you are such a wimp! You have a bad feeling about going to the movies!"

"Only *scary* movies," he mumbled.

"You're ten years old," I said sharply. "It's time to stop being scared of your own shadow. It's just an old castle with a tower," I said, gesturing towards it. "Hundreds of tourists come here every day."

"But they used to torture people here," Eddie said, suddenly looking very pale. "They used to lock people in the Tower and let them starve to death."

"Hundreds of years ago," I told him. "They don't torture people here any more, Eddie. Now they just sell postcards."

We both gazed up at the gloomy old castle built of grey stones, darkened over time. Its two narrow towers rose up like two stiff arms at its sides.

Storm clouds hovered low over the dark towers. The bent old trees in the courtyard shivered in the wind. It didn't feel like spring. The air was heavy and cold. I felt a raindrop on my forehead. Then another on my cheek.

A perfect London day, I thought. A perfect day to visit the famous Terror Tower.

This was our first day in England, and Eddie and I had been sight-seeing all over London. Our parents had to be at a conference at our hotel. So they signed us up with a tour group, and off we went.

We toured the British Museum, walked through Harrods department store, visited Westminster Abbey and Trafalgar Square.

For lunch, we had bangers and mash (sausages and mashed potatoes) at a real English pub. Then the tour group took a great bus ride, sitting on top of a bright red double-decker bus.

London was just as I had imagined it. Big and

crowded. Narrow streets lined with little shops and jammed with those old-fashioned-looking black taxis. The pavements were filled with people from all over the world.

Of course my scaredy-cat brother was totally nervous about travelling around a strange city on our own. But I'm twelve and a lot less wimpy than he is. And I managed to keep him pretty calm.

I was totally surprised when Eddie begged to visit the Terror Tower.

Mr Starkes, our bald, red-faced tour guide, gathered the group together on the pavement. There were about twelve of us, mostly old people. Eddie and I were the only kids.

Mr Starkes gave us a choice. Another museum—or the Tower.

"The Tower! The Tower!" Eddie pleaded. "I've *got* to see the Terror Tower!"

We took a long bus ride to the outskirts of the city. The shops gave way to rows of tiny redbrick houses. Then we passed even older houses, hidden behind stooped trees and low, ivy-covered walls.

When the bus pulled to a stop, we climbed out and followed a narrow street made of bricks, worn smooth over the centuries. The street ended at a high wall. Behind the wall, the Terror Tower rose up darkly.

"Hurry, Sue!" Eddie tugged my sleeve. "We'll lose the group!"

"They'll wait for us," I told my brother. "Stop worrying, Eddie. We won't get lost."

We jogged over the old bricks and caught up with the others. Wrapping his long, black overcoat around him, Mr Starkes led the way through the entrance.

He stopped and pointed at a pile of grey stones in the large, grass-covered courtyard. "That wall was the original castle wall," he explained. "It was built by the Romans in about the year 400. London was a Roman city then."

Only a small section of the wall still stood. The rest had crumbled or fallen. I couldn't believe I was staring at a wall that was over fifteen hundred years old!

We followed Mr Starkes along the path that led to the castle and its towers. "This was built by the Romans to be a walled fort," the tour guide told us. "After the Romans left, it became a prison. That started many years of cruelty and torture within these walls."

I pulled my little camera from my coat pocket and took a picture of the Roman wall. Then I turned and snapped a few pictures of the castle. The sky had darkened even more. I hoped the pictures would come out.

"This was London's first debtor's prison," Mr Starkes explained as he led the way. "If you were

132

too poor to pay your bills, you were sent to prison. Which meant that you could *never* pay your bills! So you stayed in prison for ever."

We passed a small guardhouse. It was about the size of a phone booth, made of white stones, with a slanted roof. I thought it was empty. But to my surprise, a grey-uniformed guard stepped out of it, a rifle perched stiffly on his shoulder.

I turned back and gazed at the dark wall that surrounded the castle grounds. "Look, Eddie," I whispered. "You can't see any of the city outside the wall. It's as if we really have stepped back in time."

He shivered. I don't know if it was because of my words or because of the sharp wind that blew through the old courtyard.

The castle cast a deep shadow over the path. Mr Starkes led us up to a narrow entrance at the side. Then he stopped and turned back to the group.

I was startled by the tense, sorrowful expression on his face. "I am so sorry to give you this bad news," he said, his eyes moving slowly from one of us to the next.

"Huh? Bad news?" Eddie whispered, moving closer to me.

"You will all be imprisoned in the north tower," Mr Starkes announced sternly. "There you will be tortured until you tell us the real reason why you chose to come here."

Eddie let out a startled cry. Other members of the tour group uttered shocked gasps.

Mr Starkes began to chuckle as a grin spread over his round, red face. "Just a little Terror Tower joke," he said brightly. "I've got to have *some* fun, you know."

We all laughed, too. Except Eddie. He still seemed shaken. "That guy is crazy!" Eddie whispered.

Actually, Mr Starkes was a very good tour guide. Very cheerful and helpful, and he seemed to know *everything* about London. My only problem was that sometimes I had trouble understanding his British accent.

"As you can see, the castle consists of several buildings," Mr Starkes explained, turning serious. "That long, low building over there served as a barracks for the soldiers." He pointed across the broad lawn.

I snapped a picture of the old barracks. It

looked like a long, low hut. Then I turned and snapped a picture of the grey-uniformed guard standing to attention in front of the small guardhouse.

I heard several gasps of surprise behind me. Turning back, I saw a large hooded man creep out of the entrance and sneak up behind Mr Starkes. He wore an ancient-looking green tunic and carried an enormous battleaxe.

An executioner!

He raised the battleaxe behind Mr Starkes.

"Does anyone here need a very fast haircut?" Mr Starkes asked casually, without turning around. "This is the castle barber!"

We all laughed. The man in the green executioner's costume took a quick bow, then disappeared back into the building.

"This is fun," Eddie whispered. But I noticed he was clinging very close to me.

"We are going to enter the torture chamber first," Mr Starkes announced. "Please stick together." He raised a red pennant on a long stick. "I'll carry this high so you can find me easily. It's so easy to get lost inside. There are hundreds of chambers and secret passages."

"Wow! Cool!" I exclaimed.

Eddie glanced at me doubtfully.

"You're not too scared to go into the torture chamber, are you?" I asked him.

"Who? Me?" he replied shakily.

135

"You will see some very unusual torture devices," Mr Starkes continued. "The wardens had many ways to inflict pain on their poor prisoners. We recommend that you do not try them at home."

A few people laughed. I couldn't wait to get inside.

"I ask you again to stick together," Mr Starkes urged as the group began to file through the narrow doorway into the castle. "My last tour group was lost for ever in there. Most of them are still wandering the dark chambers. My boss really scolded me when I got back to the office!"

I laughed at his lame joke. He had probably told it a thousand times.

At the entrance, I raised my eyes to the top of the dark tower. It was solid stone. No windows except for a tiny square one near the very top.

People were actually imprisoned here, I thought. Real people. Hundreds of years ago. I suddenly wondered if the castle was haunted.

I tried to read the serious expression on my brother's face. I wondered if Eddie was having the same chilling thoughts.

We stepped up to the dark entranceway. "Turn around, Eddie," I said. I took a step back and pulled my camera from my coat pocket.

"Let's go in," Eddie pleaded. "The others are getting ahead of us."

"I just want to take your picture at the castle entrance," I said.

I raised the camera to my eye. Eddie made a dumb face. I pressed the shutter release and snapped the picture.

I had no way of knowing that it was the last picture I would ever take of Eddie.

Mr Starkes led the way down a narrow stairway. Our trainers squeaked on the stone floor as we stepped into a large, dimly lit chamber.

I took a deep breath and waited for my eyes to adjust to the darkness. The air smelled old and dusty.

It was surprisingly warm inside. I unzipped my coat and pulled my long brown hair out from under the collar.

I could see several display cases against the wall. Mr Starkes led the way to a large wooden structure in the centre of the room. The group huddled closely around him.

"This is the Rack," he proclaimed, waving his red pennant at it.

"Wow. It's real!" I whispered to Eddie. I'd seen big torture devices like this in movies and comic books. But I never thought they really existed.

"The prisoner was forced to lie down here," Mr Starkes continued. "His arms and legs were strapped down. When that big wheel was turned, the ropes pulled his arms and legs, stretching them tight." He pointed to the big wooden wheel.

"Turn the wheel more, and the ropes pulled tighter," Mr Starkes said, his eyes twinkling merrily. "Sometimes the wheel was turned and the prisoner was stretched and stretched— until his bones were pulled right out of their sockets."

He chuckled. "I believe that is what is called doing a *long stretch* in prison!"

Some of the group members laughed at Mr Starkes' joke. But Eddie and I exchanged solemn glances.

Staring at the long wooden contraption with its thick ropes and straps, I pictured someone lying there. I imagined the creak of the wheel turning. And the ropes pulling tighter and tighter.

Glancing up, my eye caught a dark figure standing on the other side of the Rack. He was very tall and very broad. Dressed in a long black cape, he had pulled a wide-brimmed hat down over his forehead, hiding most of his face in shadow.

His eyes glowed darkly out from the shadow. Was he staring at me?

I poked Eddie. "See that man over there? The one in black?" I whispered. "Is he in our group?"

Eddie shook his head. "I've never seen him before," he whispered back. "He's weird! Why is he staring at us like that?"

The big man pulled the hat lower. His eyes disappeared beneath the wide brim. His black cape swirled as he stepped back into the shadows.

Mr Starkes continued to talk about the Rack. He asked if there were any volunteers to try it out. Everyone laughed.

I've got to get a picture of this thing, I decided. My friends will really think it's cool.

I reached into my coat pocket for my camera.

"Hey—!" I cried out in surprise.

I searched the other pocket. Then I searched my jeans pockets.

"I don't believe this!" I cried.

The camera was gone.

140

"Eddie—my camera!" I exclaimed. "Did you see—?"

I stopped when I saw the mischievous grin on my brother's face.

He held up his hand—with my camera in it—and his grin grew wider. "The Mad Pickpocket strikes again!" he declared.

"You took it from my pocket?" I wailed. I gave him a hard shove that sent him stumbling into the Rack.

He burst out laughing. Eddie thinks he's the world's greatest pickpocket. That's his hobby. Really. He practises all the time.

"Fastest hands on Earth!" he bragged, waving the camera at me.

I grabbed it away from him. "You're obnoxious," I told him.

I don't know why he enjoys being a thief so much. But he really is good at it. When he slid that camera from my coat pocket,

141

I didn't feel a thing.

I started to tell him to keep his hands off my camera. But Mr Starkes motioned for the group to follow him into the next room.

As Eddie and I hurried to keep up, I glimpsed the man in the black cape. He was lumbering up behind us, his face still hidden under the wide brim of his hat.

I felt a stab of fear in my chest. Was the strange man watching Eddie and me? Why?

No. He was probably just another tourist visiting the Tower. So why did I have the frightening feeling he was following us?

I kept glancing back at him as Eddie and I studied the displays of torture devices in the next room. The man didn't seem interested in the displays at all. He kept near the wall, his black cape fading into the deep shadows, his eyes straight ahead—on us!

"Look at these!" Eddie urged, pushing me towards a display shelf. "What are these?"

"Thumbscrews," Mr Starkes replied, stepping up behind us. He picked one up. "It looks like a ring," he explained. "See? It slides down over your thumb like this."

He slid the wide metal ring over his thumb. Then he raised his hand so we could see clearly. "There is a screw in the side of the ring. Turn the screw, and it digs its way into your thumb. Keep turning it, and it digs deeper and deeper."

"Ouch!" I declared.

"Very nasty," Mr Starkes agreed, setting the thumbscrew back on the display shelf. "This is a whole room of very nasty items."

"I can't believe people were actually tortured with this stuff," Eddie murmured. His voice trembled. He really didn't like scary things—especially when they were real.

"Wish I had a pair of these to use on *you*!" I teased. Eddie is such a wimp. Sometimes I can't help myself. I have to give him a hard time.

I reached behind the rope barrier and picked up a pair of metal handcuffs. They were heavier than I imagined. And they had a jagged row of metal spikes all around the inside.

"Sue—put those down!" Eddie whispered frantically.

I slipped one around my wrist. "See, Eddie, when you clamp it shut, the jagged spikes cut into your wrist," I told him.

I let out a startled gasp as the heavy metal cuff clicked shut.

"Ow!" I screamed, tugging frantically at it. "Eddie—help! I can't get it off! It's cutting me! It's cutting me!"

"Ohhhh." A horrified moan escaped Eddie's throat as he gaped at the cuff around my wrist. His mouth dropped open, and his chin started to quiver.

"Help me!" I wailed, thrashing my arm frantically, tugging at the chain. "Get me out of this!"

Eddie turned as white as a ghost.

I couldn't keep a straight face any longer. I started to laugh. And I slid the handcuff off my wrist.

"Gotcha back!" I jeered. "That's for stealing my camera. Now we're even!"

"I—I—I—" Eddie spluttered. His dark eyes glowered at me angrily. "I really thought you were hurt," he muttered. "Don't do that again, Sue. I mean it."

I stuck my tongue out at him. I know it wasn't very mature. My brother doesn't always bring out the best in me.

"Follow me, please!" Mr Starkes' voice echoed off the stone walls. Eddie and I moved closer as our tour group huddled around Mr Starkes.

"We're going to climb the stairs to the north tower now," the tour guide announced. "As you will see, the stairs are quite narrow and steep. So we will have to go single file. Please watch your step."

Mr Starkes ducked his bald head as he led the way through a low, narrow doorway. Eddie and I were at the end of the line.

The stone stairs twisted up the Tower like a corkscrew. There was no handrail. And the stairs were so steep and so twisty, I had to hold on to the wall to keep my balance as I climbed.

The air grew warmer as we made our way higher. So many feet had climbed these ancient stones, the stairs were worn smooth, the edges round.

I tried to imagine prisoners being marched up these stairs to the Tower. Their legs must have trembled with fear.

Up ahead, Eddie made his way slowly, peering up at the soot-covered stone walls. "It's too dark," he complained, turning back to me. "Hurry up, Sue. Don't get too far behind."

My coat brushed against the stone wall as I climbed. I'm pretty skinny, but the stairway

145

was so narrow, I kept bumping the sides.

After climbing for what seemed like hours, we stopped on a landing. Straight ahead of us was a small dark cell behind metal bars.

"This is a cell in which political prisoners were held," Mr Starkes told us. "Enemies of the king were brought here. You can see it was not the most comfortable place in the world."

Moving closer, I saw that the cell contained only a small stone bench and a wooden writing table.

"What happened to these prisoners?" a white-haired woman asked Mr Starkes. "Did they stay in this cell for years and years?"

"No," Mr Starkes replied, rubbing his chin. "Most of them were beheaded."

I felt a chill at the back of my neck. I stepped up to the bars and peered into the small cell.

Real people stood inside this cell, I thought. Real people held on to these bars and stared out. Sat at that little writing table. Paced back and forth in that narrow space. Waiting to meet their fate.

Swallowing hard, I glanced at my brother. I could see that he was just as horrified as I was.

"We have not reached the top of the Tower yet," Mr Starkes announced. "Let us continue our climb."

The stone steps became steeper as we made our way up the curving stairway. I trailed my hand along the wall as I followed Eddie up to the top.

And as I climbed, I suddenly had the strangest feeling—that I had been here before. That I had followed the twisting stairs. That I had climbed to the top of this ancient tower before.

Of course, that was impossible.

Eddie and I had never been to England before in our lives.

The feeling stayed with me as our tour group crowded into the tiny chamber at the top. Had I seen this tower in a movie? Had I seen pictures of it in a magazine?

Why did it look so familiar to me?

I shook my head hard, as if trying to shake away the strange, troubling thoughts. Then I stepped up beside Eddie and gazed around the tiny room.

A small round window high above our heads allowed a wash of gloomy grey light to filter down over us. The rounded walls were bare, lined with cracks and dark stains. The ceiling was low, so low that Mr Starkes and some of the other adults had to duck their heads.

"Perhaps you can feel the sadness in this room," Mr Starkes said softly.

We all huddled closer to hear him better.

Eddie stared up at the window, his expression solemn.

"This is the tower room where a young prince and princess were brought," Mr Starkes continued, speaking solemnly. "It was the early fifteenth century. The prince and princess—Edward and Susannah of York—were locked in this tiny tower cell."

He waved the red pennant in a circle. We all followed it, gazing around the small, cold room. "Imagine. Two children. Grabbed away from their home. Locked away in the drab chill of this cell in the top of a tower." Mr Starkes' voice remained just above a whisper.

I suddenly felt cold. I zipped my coat back up. Eddie had his hands shoved deep in his jeans pockets. His eyes grew wide with fear as he gazed around the tiny, dark room.

"The prince and princess weren't up here for long," Mr Starkes continued, lowering the pennant to his side. "That night while they slept, the Lord High Executioner and his men crept up the stairs. Their orders were to smother the two children. To keep the prince and princess from ever taking the throne."

Mr Starkes shut his eyes and bowed his head. The silence in the room seemed to grow heavy.

No one moved. No one spoke.

The only sound was the whisper of wind through the tiny window above our heads.

I shut my eyes, too. I tried to picture a boy and a girl. Frightened and alone. Trying to sleep in this cold, stone room.

The door bursts open. Strange men break in. They don't say a word. They rush to smother the boy and girl.

Right in this room.

Right where I am standing now, I thought.

I opened my eyes. Eddie was gazing at me, his expression troubled. "This is . . . really scary," he whispered.

"Yeah," I agreed. Mr Starkes started to tell us more.

But the camera fell out of my hand. It clattered noisily on the stone floor. I bent to pick it up. "Oh, look, Eddie—the lens has broken!" I cried.

"Ssshhh! I missed what Mr Starkes said about the prince and princess!" Eddie protested.

"But my camera—!" I shook it. I don't know why. It's not like shaking it would help fix the lens.

"What did he say? Did you hear?" Eddie demanded.

I shook my head. "Sorry. I missed it."

We walked over to a low bed against the wall. A three-legged wooden stool stood beside it. The only furniture in the chamber.

Did the prince and princess sit here? I wondered.

149

Did they stand on the bed and try to see out of that window?

What did they talk about? Did they wonder what was going to happen to them? Did they talk about the fun things they would do when they were freed? When they returned home?

It was all so sad, so horribly sad.

I stepped up to the bed and rested my hand on it. It felt hard.

Black markings on the wall caught my eye. Writing?

Had the prince or the princess left a message on the wall?

I leaned over the bed and squinted at the markings.

No. No message. Just cracks in the stone.

"Sue—come on," Eddie urged. He tugged my arm.

"Okay, okay," I replied impatiently. I ran my hand over the bed again. It felt so lumpy and hard, so uncomfortable.

I gazed up at the window. The grey light had darkened to black. Dark as night out there.

The stone walls suddenly seemed to close in on me. I felt as if I were in a dark closet, a cold, frightening closet. I imagined the walls squeezing in, choking me, smothering me.

Is that how the prince and princess felt?

Was I feeling the same fear they had known over five hundred years ago?

150

With a heavy sigh, I let go of the bed and turned to Eddie. "Let's get out of here," I said in a trembling voice. "This room is just too frightening, too sad."

We turned away from the bed, took a few steps towards the stairs—and stopped.

"Hey—!" we both cried out in surprise.

Mr Starkes and the tour group had disappeared.

"Where did they go?" Eddie cried in a shrill, startled voice. "They *left* us here!"

"They must be on their way back down the stairs," I told him. I gave him a gentle push. "Let's go."

Eddie lingered close to me. "You go first," he insisted quietly.

"You're not scared—are you?" I teased. "All alone in the Terror Tower?"

I don't know why I enjoy teasing my little brother so much. I *knew* he was scared. I was a little scared, too. But I couldn't help it.

As I said, Eddie doesn't always bring out the best in me.

I led the way to the twisting stairs. As I peered down, they seemed even darker and steeper.

"Why didn't we hear them leave?" Eddie demanded. "Why did they leave so fast?"

"It's late," I told him. "I think Mr Starkes was eager to get everyone on the bus and back to their hotels. The Tower closes at five, I think." I glanced at my watch. It was five-twenty.

"Hurry," Eddie pleaded. "I don't want to be locked in. This place gives me the creeps."

"Me, too," I confessed.

Squinting into the darkness, I started down the steps. My trainers slid on the smooth stone. Once again, I pressed one hand against the wall. It helped me keep my balance on the curving stairs.

"Where *are* they?" Eddie demanded nervously. "Why can't we hear the others on the stairs?"

The air grew cooler as we climbed lower. A pale yellow light washed over the landing just below us.

My hand swept through something soft and sticky. Cobwebs.

Yuck.

I could hear Eddie's rapid breathing behind me. "The bus will wait for us," I told him. "Just stay calm. Mr Starkes won't drive off without us."

"*Is anybody down there?*" Eddie screamed. "*Can anybody hear me?*"

His shrill voice echoed down the narrow stone stairwell.

No reply.

"Where are the guards?" Eddie demanded.

"Eddie—please don't get worked up," I

153

pleaded. "It's late. The guards are probably closing up. Mr Starkes will be waiting for us down there. I promise you."

We stepped into the pale light of the landing. The small cell we had seen before stood against the wall.

"Don't stop," Eddie pleaded, breathing hard. "Keep going, Sue. Hurry!"

I put my hand on his shoulder to calm him. "Eddie, we'll be fine," I said soothingly. "We're almost down to the ground."

"But, look—" Eddie protested. He pointed frantically.

I saw at once what was troubling him. There were *two* stairways leading down—one to the left of the cell, and one to the right.

"That's strange," I muttered, glancing from one to the other. "I don't remember a second stairway."

"Wh-which one is the right one?" he stammered.

I hesitated. "I'm not sure," I replied. I stepped over to the one on the right and peered down. I couldn't see very far because it curved so sharply.

"Which one? Which one?" Eddie repeated.

"I don't think it matters," I told him. "I mean, they both lead *down*—right?"

I motioned for him to follow me. "Come on. I

think this is the one we took when we were climbing up."

I took one step down.

Then stopped.

I heard footsteps. Heavy footsteps. Coming *up* the stairs.

Eddie grabbed my hand. "Who's that?" he whispered.

"Probably Mr Starkes," I told him. "He must be coming back up to get us."

Eddie breathed a long sigh of relief.

"Mr Starkes—is that you?" I called down.

Silence. Except for the approaching footsteps.

"Mr Starkes?" I called in a tiny voice.

When the dark figure appeared on the stairway below, I could see at once that it wasn't our tour guide.

"Oh!" I uttered a startled cry as the huge man in the black cape stepped into view.

His face was still hidden in darkness. But his eyes glowed like burning coals as he glared up at Eddie and me from under the black, wide-brimmed hat.

"Is—is this the way down?" I stammered.

He didn't reply.

He didn't move. His eyes burned into mine.

I struggled to see his face. But he kept it hidden in the shadow of the hat, pulled low over his forehead.

I took a deep breath and tried again. "We got

155

separated from our group," I said. "They must be waiting for us. Is—is this the way down?"

Again, he didn't reply. He glared up at us menacingly.

He's so big, I realized. He blocks the entire stairway.

"Sir—?" I started. "My brother and I—"

He raised a hand. A huge hand, covered in a black glove.

He pointed at us.

"You will come with me now," he growled.

I just stared at him. I didn't understand.

"You will come now," he repeated. "I do not want to hurt you. But if you try to escape, I will have no choice."

156

Eddie let out a sharp gasp.

My mouth dropped open as the man edged closer.

And then I realized who he was. "You're a guard here—right?" I asked.

He didn't reply.

"You—you scared me," I said, letting out a shrill laugh. "I mean, that costume and everything. You work here—right?"

He stepped forward, bringing his black-gloved hands up in front of him, moving the fingers.

"I'm sorry we're here so late," I continued. "We lost our group. I guess you want to close up so you can go home."

He took another step closer. His eyes flared darkly. "You know why I am here," he snarled.

"No. I don't. I—" My words were cut off as he grabbed me by the shoulder.

"Hey—let *go* of her!" Eddie cried.

But the caped man grabbed my brother, too.

His gloved fingers dug sharply into my shoulder. "Hey—!" I cried out in pain.

He backed us against the cold stone wall.

I caught a glimpse of his face, a hard, angry face. A long, sharp nose, thin lips twisted in a snarl. And the eyes. The cold, glowing eyes.

"Let us go!" Eddie demanded bravely.

"We have to meet our group!" I told the man shrilly. "We're leaving now. You can't keep us here!"

He ignored our pleas. "Do not move," he uttered in a low growl. "Stand there. Do not try to escape."

"Listen, sir—if we've done something wrong . . ." My voice trailed off.

I watched him reach into the folds of his black cape. He struggled for a moment, then pulled something out.

At first I thought they were rubber balls. Three of them.

But as he clicked them together, I realized he was holding smooth, white stones.

What is going on here? I asked myself.

Is he crazy?

Crazy and dangerous?

"Listen, sir—" Eddie started. "We have to go now."

"Don't move!" the caped man screamed. He shoved his cape violently behind him. "Don't move—and don't make a sound. You have my final warning!"

Eddie and I exchanged frightened glances. My back against the stone wall, I tried edging slowly towards the nearest stairway.

Mumbling to himself, the man concentrated on the three smooth white stones. He piled one on top of the other.

He let out an angry cry as one of the stones fell to the floor. It bounced once and slid across the smooth floor.

This is our chance! I thought.

I shoved Eddie towards the other stairwell. "Run!" I screamed.

"Do not move!" the man bellowed, grabbing up the stone. He had a booming voice that thundered off the stone walls. "I warned you. You cannot escape me!"

My brother's eyes were bugging out of his head. But he didn't have to be told twice to run!

"Stop!" the caped man bellowed. The booming voice followed us as we scrambled down, stumbling on the twisting, curving stairs, our hands trailing against the cold stone of the tower wall.

Down, down.

Turning so fast, my head spun. But I squinted into the dim light and forced myself not to be dizzy, not to fall, not to give in to the terror that rose up over me.

My camera fell out of my coat pocket. It clattered down the stairs. I didn't stop to pick it up. It was broken, anyway.

"Keep going," I urged Eddie. "Keep going! We're almost out of here!"

Or were we?

The climb down seemed so much longer.

Our trainers slapped against the stone steps. But even louder were the heavy footsteps of the caped man behind us. His bellowed cries boomed down the narrow tower, echoed all around us— as if we were being chased by a *hundred* frightening men instead of one.

Who is he?

Why is he chasing us?

Why is he so angry?

The questions bounced through my mind as I scrambled frantically down, following the twisting stairs.

No time for answers.

The big, grey door rose up in front of us before we could stop.

Eddie and I both ran right into it.

"The exit! We—we're here!" I stammered. I could hear the rumble of the man's footsteps above us on the stairway. Coming closer. Closer.

We're out! I thought. *We're safe!*

Eddie shoved the door hard with his shoulder. Shoved it again.

He turned to me, his chin quivering in fright. "It's locked. We're locked in!"

"No!" I screamed. "Push!"

We both lowered our shoulders and pushed with all our strength.

No.

161

The door didn't budge.

The man lumbered closer. So close, we could hear his muttered words.

We're trapped, I realized.

He's caught us.

Why does he want us? What is he going to do?

"One more try," I managed to choke out.

Eddie and I turned back to the door.

"Stay there!" the caped man commanded.

But Eddie and I gave the door one more desperate shove.

And it finally moved, scraping the stone floor as it slid open partway.

Eddie sucked in his breath and pushed through the opening first. Then I squeezed through.

Panting hard, we shoved the door shut behind us. The door had a long metal bar on the outside. I slid it all the way, bolting it. Locking the caped man inside.

"We're safe!" I cried, spinning away from the door.

But we weren't outside. We were in a huge, dark room.

And a cruel voice—in the room with us—a man's voice, laughing softly—told me that we weren't out of trouble.

The laughter rose up in front of us, making us both gasp.

"You have entered the king's dungeon. Abandon all hope," the man declared.

"Who—who are you?" I cried.

But more laughter was the only reply.

A single beam of pale green light from the low ceiling broke the darkness. Huddled close to Eddie, I squinted in the eerie glow, desperate to find a way to escape.

"Over there! Look!" Eddie whispered, pointing.

Across the room, I could see a barred cell against the wall.

We crept forward a few steps. Then we saw it.

A bony hand reaching out from between the bars.

"No!" I gasped.

Eddie and I jumped back.

The pounding on the door behind us made us

both jump again. "You cannot escape!" the caped man raged from the other side of the door.

Eddie grabbed my hand as the man furiously pounded on the door. The sound boomed louder than thunder.

Would the bolt hold?

Ahead of us, two bony hands reached out from another dungeon cell.

"This can't be happening!" Eddie choked out. "There aren't any dungeons today!"

"Another doorway!" I whispered, trembling with fright as I stared at the hands poking out from the dark cells. "Find another doorway."

My eyes frantically searched the darkness. Off in a distant corner, I glimpsed a slender crack of light.

I started to run towards it—and tripped over something. Something chained to the floor.

It was a body. A body of a man sprawled on the floor. And I landed on his chest with a sickening *thud*.

The chains rattled loudly as my foot tangled in them.

My knees and elbows hit the stone floor hard. Pain shot through my entire body.

The old man didn't move.

I scrambled up. Stared down at him.

And realized he was a dummy.

Not real. Just a dummy, chained to the floor.

"Eddie—it's not real!" I cried.

164

"Huh?" He stared at me, his face twisted in confusion, in fright.

"It's not real! None of it!" I repeated. "Look! The hands in the dungeon cells—they're not moving! It's all a display, Eddie. Just a display!"

Eddie started to reply. But the cruel laughter interrupted him.

"You have entered the king's dungeon. Abandon all hope," the voice repeated. Then more evil laughter.

Just a tape. Just a recording.

There wasn't anyone in the room with us. No dungeon keeper.

I let out a long sigh. My heart was still pounding like a bass drum. But I felt a little better knowing that we weren't trapped in a real dungeon.

"We're okay," I assured Eddie.

And then the door burst open with a loud *crack*. And the big man roared into the room, his cape fluttering behind him, his dark eyes glowing in victory.

Eddie and I froze in the middle of the floor.

The caped man froze, too. The only sound was his harsh, raspy breathing.

We stared through the dim light at each other. Frozen like the dummies in the cells.

"You cannot escape," the man growled once again. "You know you will not leave the castle."

His words sent a cold shiver down my back.

"Leave us alone!" Eddie pleaded in a tiny voice.

"What do you want?" I demanded. "Why are you chasing us?"

The big man pressed his gloved hands against his waist. "You know the answer," he replied flatly. He took a step towards Eddie and me. "Are you ready to come with me now?" he demanded.

I didn't reply. Instead, I leaned close to Eddie and whispered, "Get ready to run."

Eddie continued to stare straight ahead. He didn't blink or nod his head. I couldn't tell if he had even heard me.

"You know you have no choice," the man said softly. He reached both hands into the folds of his cape. Once again, he pulled out the mysterious white stones. And once again, I caught a glimpse of his dark eyes, saw the cold sneer on his lips.

"You—you've made a mistake!" Eddie stammered.

The man shook his head. The wide brim of the black hat cast tilting shadows on the floor. "I have made no mistake. Do not run from me again. You know you must come with me now."

Eddie and I didn't need a signal.

Without saying a word to each other, without *glancing* at each other, we spun around—and started to run.

The man shouted in protest and took off after us.

The room seemed to stretch on for ever. It must be the entire basement of the castle, I realized.

Beyond the beam of light, the darkness rose up like fog.

My fear weighed me down. My legs felt as if they were a thousand pounds each.

I'm moving in slow motion, I thought, struggling to speed up. Eddie and I are crawling like turtles.

167

He'll catch us. He'll catch us in two seconds.

I glanced back when I heard the caped man cry out. He had tripped over the same dummy chained to the floor. He had fallen heavily.

As he scrambled to his feet, my eyes searched the far wall for a door. Or a hallway. Or any kind of opening.

"How—how do we get *out* of here?" Eddie cried. "We're trapped, Sue!"

"No!" I cried. I spotted a worktable against the wall. Cluttered with tools. I searched for something to use as a weapon. Didn't see anything. Grabbed a torch, instead.

Frantically pushed the button.

Would it work?

Yes.

A white beam of light darted over the floor. I raised it to the far wall. "Eddie—look!" I whispered.

A low opening in the wall. Some kind of tunnel? A tunnel we could escape through?

In another second, we were ducking our heads and stepping into the dark opening.

I kept my light ahead of us, down at our feet. We had to stoop as we ran. The tunnel was curved at the top, and not high enough for us to stand.

The tunnel ran straight for a while, then curved down and to the right. The air felt damp and cool. I could hear the trickle of water nearby.

168

"It's an old sewer," I told Eddie. "That means it has to lead us out somewhere."

"I hope so," Eddie replied breathlessly.

Running hard, we followed the curve of the sewer. My light leaped about, jumping from the low ceiling to the damp stone floor.

The light revealed wide metal rungs hanging from the ceiling. Eddie and I had to duck even lower to keep from smashing our heads against them.

The light from my torch bounced wildly from the floor to the rungs along the top of the sewer. Eddie and I splashed through puddles of dirty water.

We both gasped when we heard the footsteps behind us.

Heavy, ringing footsteps. Thundering in the low tunnel. Growing louder. Louder.

I glanced back. But the caped man was hidden by the curve of the sewer tunnel.

His footsteps boomed steadily, rapidly. I could tell he wasn't far behind.

He's going to catch us, I told myself in a panic.

This tunnel is never going to end.

Eddie and I can't run much farther.

He's going to catch us in this dark, damp sewer.

And then what?

What does he want?

Why did he say that we *knew* what he wanted? How could we know?

I stumbled forward. The torch bumped against the wall and fell from my hand.

It clattered to the tunnel floor and rolled in front of me.

The light shone back into the tunnel, back towards the caped man.

I saw him move into view, bent low, running hard.

"Ohhh." A frightened moan escaped my lips.

I bent to pick up the torch. It slid out of my trembling hand.

That was all the time the caped man needed.

He grabbed Eddie with both hands. He pulled the black cape around my brother, trapping him.

Then he reached for me. "I told you—there is no escape," he rasped.

I ducked out of the caped man's grasp.

With another frightened groan, I grabbed the torch off the floor.

I planned to use it as a weapon. To shine it in the caped man's eyes. Or swing it at his head.

But I didn't get a chance.

I froze in horror as the beam of light bounced down the tunnel—and I saw the rats.

Hundreds of them. Hundreds of chittering grey rats.

The darting light made their eyes glow red as fire. The rats came scrabbling over the sewer floor. Snapping their jaws hungrily, gnashing their jagged teeth as they came charging at us.

Their shrill whistling and chittering echoed through the tunnel. The terrifying sound made my breath catch in my throat.

The tiny red eyes glowed in the light as they

scrabbled towards us. As they pulled their scrawny bodies over the hard floor, their tails slithered behind them like dark snakes.

The caped man saw them, too. He leaped back in surprise.

And Eddie came tearing out from under the cape. He gulped in shock as his eyes locked on the charging rats.

"Jump!" I cried. "Eddie—jump!"

Eddie didn't move. We both gaped at the rats in horror. A churning sea of whistling, chewing, red-eyed rats. A living tidal wave of rats.

"Jump! Jump—now!" I shrieked.

I raised both hands. Jumped.

Eddie jumped, too. We grabbed on to the metal bars embedded in the sewer roof.

Pulling myself up, I frantically lifted my feet as high as I could from the floor.

Higher. Higher. As the rats charged underneath me.

A foul odour rose up, nearly choking me as the rats ran past.

I could hear the *tap tap tap* of their claws against the floor. Hear the *swish* of their sweeping tails.

I couldn't see the rats in the darkness. But I could hear them. And feel them. They jumped at my shoes. Scratched at my legs with their sharp claws. And kept coming.

172

I turned to see the caped man start to run back.

He stumbled with lurching steps as he tried to flee the thundering wave of rats. His arms shot forward as if reaching for safety. The black cape whipped up behind him.

The wide-brimmed hat flew off his head and floated to the floor. A dozen rats pounced on it, climbed all over it, and began chewing it to pieces.

The man's footsteps echoed in the tunnel as he ran faster. Rats leaped up at his cape, clawing it, snapping their jaws, and shrieking excitedly.

A second later, he disappeared around the curve of the sewer.

The rats scrambled noisily after him. As they vanished around the curve, the sounds all blended together, became a roar, a roar that rang through the long sewer.

A roar of horror.

Both my arms were aching, throbbing with pain. But I kept my feet high off the floor. I didn't let go of the metal rung until I was sure all the rats had disappeared.

The roar faded into the distance.

I heard Eddie's heavy breathing. He let out a sharp groan and dropped to the floor.

I let go of the bar and lowered myself, too. I waited for my heart to stop pounding, for

173

the blood to stop throbbing at my temples.

"That was a close call," Eddie murmured. His chin trembled. His face was as grey as the tunnel walls.

I shuddered. I knew I'd see the hundreds of tiny red eyes in my dreams, hear the clicking of their long claws and the *swish* of their scraggly tails.

"Let's get out of this disgusting sewer!" I cried. "Mr Starkes must be frantic searching for us."

Eddie picked up the torch and handed it to me. "I can't wait to get back on the tour bus," he said. "I can't wait to get away from this awful tower. I can't believe we've been chased by a crazy person through a sewer. This can't really be happening to us, Sue!"

"It's happening," I declared, shaking my head. I suddenly had another thought. "Mum and Dad are probably out of their meeting," I said. "They're probably worried sick about us."

"Not as worried as I am!" Eddie exclaimed.

I beamed the light ahead, keeping it down on the sewer floor, and we started walking. The tunnel floor rose up and curved to the left. We started to climb.

"There's *got* to be an end to this sewer," I muttered. "It's *got* to end somewhere!"

A faint roar up ahead made me cry out.

More rats!

Eddie and I both stopped. And listened.

"Hey—!" I uttered excitedly when I realized it was a different sound.

The sound of wind rushing into the tunnel.

That meant we had to be close to the end. And that the sewer emptied somewhere *outside*.

"Let's go!" I cried excitedly. The beam of light bounced ahead of us as we started to run.

The tunnel curved again. And then suddenly ended.

I saw a metal ladder, reaching straight up. Straight up to a large, round hole in the tunnel ceiling. Gazing up at the hole, I saw the night sky.

Eddie and I let out shouts of joy. He scrambled up the ladder, and I pulled myself up right behind him.

It was a cold, damp night. But we didn't care. The air smelled so fresh and clean.

And we were out. Out of the sewer. Out of the Terror Tower.

Away from that frightening man in the black cape.

I gazed around quickly, trying to figure out where we were. The Tower tilted up above us, a black shadow against the blue-black sky.

The lights had all been turned off. The tiny guardhouse lay dark and empty. Not another soul in sight.

I saw the low wall that divided the Tower from the rest of the world. And then I found the stone path that led to the exit and the car park.

Our shoes thudded over the smooth stones as we hurried towards the car park. A pale half-moon slid out from behind wispy clouds. It cast a shimmering silver light over the whispering trees and the long stone wall.

It all suddenly looked unreal.

Without stopping, I glanced back at the old castle. The moonlight shone off the jutting towers, as if casting them in a pale spotlight.

Real people walked on this path hundreds of years ago, I thought.

And real people died up in that tower.

With a shiver, I turned back and kept jogging. Eddie and I moved through the open gate and out past the wall.

We're back in modern times, I thought. Back where we are safe.

But our happiness didn't last long.

The car park shimmered darkly in the pale moonlight. Empty.

The tour bus was gone.

Eddie and I both turned to search up and down the street. The long, empty street.

"They left us," Eddie murmured with a sigh. "How are we going to get back to the hotel?"

I started to answer—but stopped when I saw the man.

A tall, white-haired man, limping towards us, moving fast, pointing and calling, "You there! You there!"

Oh, no, I thought wearily, feeling my body freeze in fear.

Now what?

"You there! You there!"

The man's shoulder dipped in the big, grey overcoat he wore as he charged at us, limping with each step.

Eddie and I huddled close together, staring back at him as he hurried across the empty car park. His white hair tumbled out from under a small grey cap. The overcoat hung down nearly to his ankles and bulged over his skinny frame.

He stepped up in front of us and waited to catch his breath. His tiny eyes caught the moonlight as he narrowed them at us, studying Eddie, then me.

"Are you the two kids that bus driver was looking for?" he asked in a shrill, high voice. He had a different accent from Mr Starkes'. I think it was Scottish.

Eddie and I nodded.

"Well, I'm the night guard here," the man told

us. "There's no one here but me after closing."

"Uh . . . where is our bus?" Eddie asked quietly.

"It left," the man replied sharply. "He searched everywhere for you. But he couldn't wait any longer. What happened? Did you get lost in there?" He motioned back towards the Tower.

"A man chased us," Eddie replied breathlessly. "He said we had to come with him. He was really scary, and—"

"Man? What man?" The night guard eyed us suspiciously.

"The man in the black cape!" I replied. "And the black hat. He chased us. In the Tower."

"There's no man in the Tower," the guard replied, shaking his head. "I told you. I'm the only one here after closing."

"But he's in there!" I cried. "He chased us! He was going to hurt us! He chased us through the sewer and the rats—"

"Sewer? What were you two doing in the sewer?" the guard demanded. "We have rules here about where tourists are allowed. If you break the rules, we can't be responsible."

He sighed. "Now you come out here with a wild story about a man in a black cape. And running through the sewers. Wild stories. Wild stories."

Eddie and I exchanged glances. We could both see that this man wasn't going to believe us.

"How do we get back to our hotel?" Eddie

asked. "Our parents will be really worried."

I glanced at the street. There were no cars or buses in sight.

"Do you have any money?" the guard asked, replacing his cap. "There's a phone box on the corner. I can call for a taxi."

I reached into my jeans pocket and felt the heavy coins my parents had given me before Eddie and I set out on the tour. Then I breathed a long sigh of relief.

"We have money," I told the guard.

"It'll cost you at least fifteen or twenty pounds from way out here," he warned.

"That's OK," I replied. "Our parents gave us English money. If we don't have enough, my parents will pay the driver."

He nodded. Then he turned to Eddie. "You look all done in, lad. Did you get frightened up in that tower?"

Eddie swallowed hard. "I just want to get back to our hotel," he murmured.

The guard nodded. Then, tucking his hands into the pockets of the big overcoat, he led the way to the phone booth.

The black taxi pulled up about ten minutes later. The driver was a young man with long, wavy blond hair. "What hotel?" he asked, leaning out of the passenger window.

"The Barclay," I told him.

180

Eddie and I climbed into the back. It was warm in the taxi. It felt so great to sit down!

As we pulled away from the Terror Tower, I didn't glance back. I never wanted to see that old castle again.

The car rolled smoothly through the dark streets. The taxi meter clicked pleasantly. The driver hummed to himself.

I shut my eyes and leaned my head back against the leather seat. I tried not to think about the frightening man who had chased us in the Tower. But I couldn't force him from my mind.

Soon we were back in the centre of London. Cars and taxis jammed the streets. We passed brightly lit theatres and restaurants.

The taxi pulled up to the front of the Barclay Hotel and eased to a stop. The driver slid open the window behind his seat and turned to me. "That'll be fifteen pounds, sixty pence."

Eddie sat up drowsily. He blinked several times, surprised to see that we had reached our destination.

I pulled the big, heavy coins from my pocket. I held them up to the driver. "I don't really know what is what," I confessed. "Can you take the right amount from these?"

The driver glanced at the coins in my hands, sniffed, then raised his eyes to me. "What are those?" he asked coldly.

"Coins," I replied. I didn't know what else to say. "Do I have enough to pay you?"

He stared back at me. "Do you have any *real* money? Or are you going to pay me with play money?"

"I—I don't understand," I stammered. My hand started to tremble, and I nearly dropped the coins.

"I don't either," the driver replied sharply. "But I do know that those aren't real coins. We use English pounds here, miss."

His expression turned angry. He glared at me through the little window in the glass partition. "Now, are you going to pay me in English pounds, or are we going to have some major trouble? I want my money—now!"

I pulled the coins away from him and raised them close to my face. It was dark in the back of the taxi, and hard to see.

The coins were large and round. They felt heavy, made of real gold or silver. It was too dark to read the words on them.

"Why would my parents give me play money?" I asked the driver.

He shrugged. "I don't know your parents."

"Well, they will pay you the fifteen pounds," I told him. I struggled to shove the big coins back into my pocket.

"Fifteen pounds, sixty—plus tip," the driver said, frowning at me. "Where are your parents? In the hotel?"

I nodded. "Yes. They were at a meeting in the hotel. But they're probably up in the room now. We'll get them to come down and pay you."

"In real money, if you please," the driver said,

rolling his eyes. "If they're not down here in five minutes, I'll come in after you."

"They'll be right down. I promise," I told him.

I pushed open the door and scrambled out of the cab. Eddie followed me on to the pavement, shaking his head. "This is weird," he muttered.

A red-uniformed doorman held the hotel door open for us, and we hurried into the huge, chandeliered lobby. Most people seemed to be heading the other way, going out for dinner, I guessed.

My stomach grumbled. I suddenly realized I was starving.

Eddie and I made our way past the long front desk. We were walking so fast, we nearly collided with a porter pushing a big trolley stacked high with suitcases.

To our right, I could hear dishes clattering in the hotel restaurant. The aroma of fresh-baked bread floated in the air.

The lift doors opened. A red-haired woman in a fur coat stepped off, walking a white toy poodle. Eddie got tangled in the lead. I had to pull him free so we wouldn't miss the lift.

We stumbled into the lift. As the doors slid shut, I pushed Six. "What was wrong with that money?" Eddie asked.

I shrugged. "I don't know. I guess Dad made a mistake."

The doors slid open on Six, and we hurried

184

side by side down the long, carpeted hall to our room.

I stepped around a room service tray on the floor. Someone had left half a sandwich and part of a bowl of fruit. My stomach rumbled again, reminding me how hungry I was.

"Here we are." Eddie ran up to the door to room 626 and knocked. "Hey, Mum! Dad! It's us!"

"Open up!" I called impatiently.

Eddie knocked again, a little louder. "Hey—!"

We pressed our ears close to the door and listened.

Silence. No footsteps. No voices.

"Hey—are you in there?" Eddie called. He knocked again. "Hurry up! It's us!"

He turned to me. "They *must* be out of that meeting by now," he muttered.

I cupped my hands around my mouth. "Mum? Dad? Are you there?" I called in.

No reply.

Eddie's shoulders slumped, and he let out an unhappy sigh. "Now what?"

"Are you having trouble?" a woman's voice asked.

I turned to see a hotel maid. She wore a grey uniform and a small white cap over her short, dark hair. She had been pushing a trolley loaded with towels. She stopped across from Eddie and me.

185

"Our parents are still at a meeting," I told her. "My brother and I—we're locked out."

She studied us for a moment. Then she stepped away from the trolley and raised a large key-chain filled with keys.

"I'm not really supposed to do this," she said, shuffling through the clattering keys. "But I guess it's okay to let you kids in."

She put a key into the lock, turned it, and pushed open the door for us. Eddie and I both thanked her and told her she was a lifesaver. She smiled and moved on down the hall, pushing her towel trolley.

The room was dark. I clicked on the light as Eddie and I stepped in.

"They're not here," I said softly. "No sign of them."

"They probably left a note," Eddie replied. "Maybe they had to go out with people from the meeting. Or maybe they're down in the restaurant, waiting for us."

Our room was actually a suite. A front room and two bedrooms.

Turning on lights as I went, I made my way to the desk in the corner. A writing pad and pen rested in the centre of the desk. But the pad was blank. No message.

No message from Mum and Dad on the bed-side table, either.

"That's weird," Eddie muttered.

I crossed the room and stepped into their bedroom. I clicked on the ceiling light and glanced around.

The room had been made up. The bed was smooth and unwrinkled. There was no message for us anywhere. The dressing-table lay bare. No clothes tossed over a chair. No shoes on the floor. No briefcases or notepads from their meeting.

No sign that anyone had even been in the room.

I turned and saw that Eddie had moved to the wardrobe. He pushed the sliding door open all the way.

"Sue, look!" he shouted. "No clothes! Mum's and Dad's clothes—our clothes—they're all gone!"

A heavy feeling of dread started in my stomach and weighted down my entire body. "What is going *on* here?" I cried.

"They wouldn't just leave!" I exclaimed. I walked over to the wardrobe and checked it out for myself. I don't know what I expected to see. It was clear from across the room that the wardrobe was completely empty.

"Are you sure we're in the right room?" Eddie asked. He pulled open the top drawer of the dressing table. Empty.

"Of course this is the right room," I replied impatiently.

Eddie pulled out the rest of the drawers. They were all empty.

We searched every inch of the room. No sign of Mum and Dad.

"We'd better go down to the desk," I suggested, thinking hard. "We'll find out what room the meeting is being held in. Then we'll go there and talk to Mum and Dad."

"I can't believe they're still at the meeting," Eddie murmured, shaking his head. "And why would they pack up and take all our clothes to the meeting with them?"

"I'm sure there's a good answer," I said. "Come on. Let's go downstairs."

We made our way back down the long hall and took the lift to the lobby.

We found a crowd around the front desk. A large woman, dressed in a green suit, was arguing angrily about her room. "I was promised a view of the river," she screamed at the red-faced man behind the desk. "And I want a view of the river!"

"But, madam," he replied softly, "the hotel is not located near the river. We do not have any river views from this hotel."

"I must have a river view!" the woman insisted. "I have it right here in writing!" She flashed a sheet of paper in front of the man's face.

The argument continued for a few minutes more. I quickly lost interest in it. I thought about Mum and Dad. I wondered where they were. I wondered why they hadn't left us a note or a message.

Eddie and I finally got up to the desk about ten minutes later. The receptionist tucked some papers into a file, then turned to us with an automatic smile. "Can I help you?"

"We're trying to find our parents," I said, leaning my elbows on the desk. "They're in the meeting, I think. Can you tell us where the meeting is?"

He stared at me for a long moment, his face blank, as if he didn't understand. "What meeting is that?" he asked finally.

I thought hard. I couldn't remember what the meeting was called. Or what it was about.

"It's the big meeting," I replied uncertainly. "The one people came from all over the world for."

He twisted his mouth into a thoughtful pout. "Hmmm . . ."

"A very big meeting," Eddie chimed in.

"We have a problem," the receptionist said, frowning. He scratched his right ear. "There aren't any meetings in the hotel this week."

I stared back at him. My mouth dropped open. I started to say something, but the words just didn't come out.

"No meetings?" Eddie asked weakly.

The receptionist shook his head. "No meetings."

A young woman called to him from the office. He signalled to me that he'd be right back. Then he hurried over to see what she wanted.

"Are we in the right hotel?" Eddie whispered to me. I could see the worry tighten his features.

"Of course," I said sharply. "Why do you keep asking me these stupid questions? I'm not an idiot, you know. Why do you keep asking, is this the right room? Is this the right hotel?"

"Because nothing makes sense," he muttered.

I started to reply, but the receptionist returned to the desk. "May I ask your room number?" he demanded, scratching his ear again.

"Six twenty-six," I told him.

He punched several keys on his computer keyboard, then squinted at the green monitor. "I'm sorry. That room is vacant," he said.

"What?" I cried.

The receptionist studied me, narrowing his eyes. "There is no one in room 626 at the present," he repeated.

"But *we* are!" Eddie cried.

The receptionist forced a smile to his face. He raised both hands, as if to say, "Let's all remain calm."

"We will find your parents," he told us, leaving the smile frozen on his face. He punched a few computer keys. "Now, what is your last name?"

I opened my mouth to answer. But no answer came to my mind.

I glanced at Eddie. His face was knitted in concentration.

"What is your last name, kids?" the receptionist repeated. "If your parents are in the hotel, I'm sure we can track them down for you. But I need to know your last name."

I stared blankly at him.

I had a strange, tingly feeling that started at the back of my neck and ran all the way down my body. I suddenly felt as if I couldn't breathe, as if my heart had stopped.

My last name. My last name . . .

Why couldn't I remember my last name?

I could feel my body start to shake. Tears brimmed in my eyes.

This was so upsetting!

My name is Sue, I told myself. *Sue . . . Sue . . . what?*

Shaking, tears running down my cheeks, I grabbed Eddie by the shoulders. "Eddie," I demanded, "what's our last name?"

"I—I don't know!" he sobbed.

"Oh, Eddie!" I pulled my brother close and hugged him. "What's wrong with us? What's *wrong* with us?"

"We have to stay calm," I told my brother. "If we take a deep breath and just relax, I'm sure we'll be able to remember."

"I guess you're right," Eddie replied uncertainly. He stared straight ahead. He was gritting his teeth, trying hard not to cry.

It was a few minutes later. The receptionist had suggested that we go to the hotel restaurant. He promised he'd try to find our parents while we ate.

That suggestion was fine with Eddie and me. We were both starving!

We sat at a small table in the back of the restaurant. I gazed around the big, elegant room. Crystal chandeliers cast sparkling light over the well-dressed diners. On a small balcony overlooking the room, a string quartet played classical music.

Eddie tapped his hands nervously on the white tablecloth. I kept picking up the heavy silverware and twirling it in my hand.

The tables all around us were filled with laughing, happy people. Three children at the next table, very dressed up, were singing a song in French to their smiling parents.

Eddie leaned over the table and whispered to me. "How are we going to pay for the food? Our money isn't any good."

"We can charge it to the room," I replied. "When we figure out what room we're in." Eddie nodded and slouched back in his high-backed chair.

A waiter in a black tuxedo appeared beside the table. He smiled at Eddie and me. "Welcome to the Barclay," he said. "And what may I bring you this evening?"

"Could we see a menu?" I asked.

"There is no menu right now," the waiter replied, without changing his smile. "We are still serving tea."

"Only tea?" Eddie cried. "No food?"

The waiter chuckled. "Our high tea includes sandwiches, scones, croissants, and an assortment of pastries."

"Yes. We'll have that," I told him.

He gave a quick bow of his head, turned, and headed towards the kitchen.

"At least we'll get something to eat," I murmured.

Eddie didn't seem to hear me. He kept

glancing at the doorway at the front of the restaurant. I knew he was looking for Mum and Dad.

"Why can't we remember our last name?" he asked glumly.

"I don't know," I confessed. "I'm very confused."

Every time I started to think about it, I felt dizzy. I kept telling myself I was just hungry. You'll remember after you've had something to eat, I kept repeating.

The waiter brought a tray of tiny sandwiches, cut into triangles. I recognized egg salad and tuna-fish. I didn't know what the others were.

But Eddie and I didn't care. We started devouring the sandwiches as soon as the waiter set them down.

We drank two cups of tea. Then our next tray arrived with scones and croissants. We loaded them up with butter and strawberry jam, and gobbled them down hungrily.

"Maybe if we tell the man at the front desk what Mum and Dad look like, he can help us find them," Eddie suggested. He grabbed the last croissant before I could get it.

"Good idea," I said.

Then I let out a silent gasp. I had the dizzy feeling again.

"Eddie," I said, "I can't remember what Mum and Dad look like!"

195

He let the croissant fall from his hand. "I can't either," he murmured, lowering his head. "This is crazy, Sue!"

I shut my eyes. "Shhh. Just try to picture them," I urged. "Force away all other thoughts. Concentrate. Try to picture them."

"I—I can't!" Eddie stammered. I could hear the panic in his high-pitched voice. "Something is wrong, Sue. Something is very wrong with us."

I swallowed hard. I opened my eyes. I couldn't conjure up any kind of picture of my parents.

I tried thinking about Mum. Was she blonde? Red-haired? Black-haired? Was she tall? Short? Thin? Fat?

I couldn't remember.

"Where do we live?" Eddie wailed. "Do we live in a house? I can't picture it, Sue. I can't picture it at all."

His voice cracked. I could see he was having trouble holding back the tears.

Panic choked my throat. I suddenly felt as if I couldn't breathe. I stared at Eddie and couldn't say a word.

What could I say?

My brain spun like a tornado. "We've lost our memory," I finally uttered. "At least, part of our memory."

"How?" Eddie demanded in a trembling voice. "How could that happen to *both* of us?"

196

I clasped my hands tightly in my lap. My hands were as cold as ice. "At least we still remember *some* things," I said, trying not to despair completely.

"We still remember our first names," Eddie replied. "But not our last. And what else do we remember?"

"We remember our room number," I said. "Six twenty-six."

"But the desk clerk said we don't belong in that room!" Eddie cried.

"And we remember *why* we came to London," I continued. "Because Mum and Dad had these important meetings."

"But there *are* no meetings at the hotel!" Eddie exclaimed. "Our memories are wrong, Sue. They're all wrong!"

I insisted on figuring out what we *did* remember. I had the feeling if I could list what we *did* remember, we wouldn't feel so upset about what we had forgotten.

I knew it was a crazy idea. But I didn't know what else to do.

"I remember the tour we took today," I said. "I remember everywhere we went in London. I remember Mr Starkes. I remember—"

"What about yesterday?" Eddie interrupted. "What did we do yesterday, Sue?"

I started to reply, but my breath caught in my throat.

I couldn't remember yesterday!

Or the day before. Or the day before that.

"Oh, Eddie," I moaned, raising my hands to my cheeks, "something is terribly wrong."

Eddie didn't seem to hear me. His eyes were locked on the front of the restaurant.

I followed his gaze—and saw the slender, blond-haired man step into the room.

The taxi driver.

We had forgotten all about him!

198

I jumped up. The napkin fell off my lap, on to my shoe. I kicked it away and reached down to tug Eddie's arm. "Come on—let's get out of here."

Eddie gazed up at me uncertainly, then back at the taxi driver. The taxi driver had stopped just past the entrance. His eyes were searching each table.

"Hurry," I whispered. "He hasn't seen us yet."

"But maybe we should just explain to him—" Eddie said.

"Huh? Explain what?" I shot back. "That we can't pay him because we lost our memory and don't know our name? I really don't think he'll buy that—do you?"

Eddie twisted his face in a frown. "Okay. How do we get out of here?" he demanded.

The front door was blocked by the taxi driver. But I spotted a glass door on the back wall near our table.

The door had a filmy, white curtain over it and a small sign that read: NO EXIT.

But I didn't care. Eddie and I had no choice. We *had* to leave—fast!

I grabbed the knob and pulled the door open. Eddie and I slipped through, then tugged the door shut behind us.

"I don't think he saw us," I whispered. "I think we're okay."

We turned away from the door and found ourselves in a long, dark hallway. This must be an area used by the hotel workers, I thought. The floor had no carpet. The walls were dirty, stained, and unpainted.

We turned a corner. I held out a hand to stop Eddie.

We listened hard for footsteps. Had the taxi driver seen us duck out? Was he coming after us?

I couldn't hear a thing over the pounding of my heart. "What a horrible day!" I wailed.

And then the day turned even more horrible.

The man in the black cape stepped out from around the corner. "Did you really think I wouldn't follow you?" he asked. "Did you really think you could escape from *me*?"

200

He moved forward quickly, his face hidden in the shadows.

Eddie and I were trapped, our backs pressed against the curtained, glass door.

As the caped man drew near, his features came into view. His eyes were dark and cold. His mouth was locked in a menacing snarl.

He raised his palm to Eddie. "Give them back," he demanded.

Eddie's eyes bulged in surprise. "Huh? Give *what* back?" he cried.

The caped man kept his palm in front of Eddie's face. "Give them back—now!" he bellowed. "Do not play games with me."

Eddie's expression slowly changed. He glanced at me, then turned back to the caped man. "If I give them back, will you let us go?"

I was totally confused. *Give what back?* What was Eddie talking about?

The caped man uttered a short, dry laugh. It

201

sounded more like a cough. "Do you dare to bargain with me?" he asked my brother.

"Eddie—what is he *talking* about?" I cried.

But Eddie didn't reply. He kept his eyes locked on the shadowy face of the caped man. "If I give them back, will you let us go?"

"Hand them back—now," the big man replied sharply, leaning menacingly over Eddie.

Eddie sighed. He reached into his trouser pocket. And to my shock, he pulled out the three smooth, white stones.

My brother the pickpocket had struck again. "Eddie—when did you take those?" I demanded.

"In the sewer," Eddie replied. "When he grabbed me."

"But, why?" I asked.

Eddie shrugged. "I don't know. They seemed important to him. So I thought—"

"They *are* important!" the caped man bellowed. He grabbed the stones from Eddie's hand.

"Now will you let us go?" Eddie cried.

"Yes. We will go now," the man replied, concentrating on the stones.

"That's *not* what I said!" Eddie exclaimed. "Will you let us go?"

The man ignored him. He piled the stones one on top of the other in his palm. Then he chanted some words, words in a foreign language that I didn't recognize.

As soon as he chanted the words, the hallway began to shimmer. The doors began to wiggle and bend, as if made of rubber. The floor buckled and swayed.

The caped man began to shimmer and bend, too.

The hallway throbbed with a blinding, white light.

I felt a sharp stab of pain—as if I had been hit hard in the stomach.

I couldn't breathe.

Everything went black.

Flickering orange light broke the darkness.

I opened my eyes. Blinked several times. Took a deep breath.

The caped man was gone.

"Eddie—are you okay?" I asked in a quivering voice.

"I—I think so," he stammered.

I gazed down the long hall, startled to find it lit by flickering candles. A candle was perched in a holder beside each door.

"Sue, how did we get in this hallway?" Eddie asked softly. "Where is the caped man?"

"I don't know," I replied. "I'm as confused as you are."

We stepped into the flickering light. "This has to be the old section of the hotel," I guessed. "They must want it to look old-fashioned."

We walked past door after door. The long, narrow hallway was silent except for the thud of our shoes on the hardwood floor. The doors

204

were all closed. No other people in sight.

The flickering candlelight, the dark doorways, the eerie silence—all gave me a cold, tingly feeling. My entire body trembled.

We kept walking through the dim, orangey light.

"I—I want to go back to the room," Eddie stammered as we turned another corner. "Maybe Mum and Dad have come back. Maybe they're waiting for us up there."

"Maybe," I replied doubtfully.

We entered another silent hallway, glowing eerily in darting, dancing candlelight. "There's got to be a lift down here somewhere," I muttered.

But we passed only dark, closed doors.

Turning another corner, we nearly bumped into a group of people.

"Ohh!" I cried out, so startled to find others in these long, empty hallways.

I stared at them as they passed. They wore long robes, and their faces were hidden under dark hoods. I couldn't tell if they were men or women.

They moved silently, making no sound at all. They paid no attention to Eddie or me.

"Uh ... can you tell us where the lift is?" Eddie called after them.

They didn't turn back, didn't reply.

"Sirs?" Eddie called, chasing after them.

205

"Please! Have you seen the lift?"

One of them turned back towards Eddie. The others continued moving silently down the hallway, their long robes swishing softly.

I stepped up beside my brother and the robed figure. I could see the face under the hood. An old man with bushy white eyebrows.

He peered out at Eddie, then at me. His eyes were dark and wet. His expression was sorrowful.

"I smell evil around you," he croaked in a dry whisper.

"What?" I cried. "My brother and I—"

"Do not leave the abbey," the old man instructed. "I smell evil around you. Your time is near. So near. So very near . . ."

"What abbey?" I demanded. "Why are you saying that?"

The old man didn't reply. The candlelight glowed in his watery eyes. He nodded his head solemnly under the heavy hood. Then he turned away from us and glided silently after the others, the hem of his robe sweeping along the bare floor.

"What did he mean?" Eddie demanded when the hooded man had vanished around a corner. "Why did he try to frighten us?"

I shook my head. "It had to be some kind of a joke," I replied. "They're probably on their way to a party or something."

Eddie frowned thoughtfully. "They were creepy, Sue. They didn't look like they were in a party mood to me."

I sighed. "Let's find the lift and get up to the room. I don't like this old part of the hotel. It's just too dark and scary."

"Hey, I'm the one who gets scared," Eddie said, following me down the hall. "You're supposed to be the brave one—remember?"

We wandered down one long, candlelit hallway after another, feeling more and more lost. We couldn't find a lift or stairs or any kind of exit.

"Are we going to walk for ever?" Eddie whined. "There *has* to be a way out of here—doesn't there?"

"Let's go back," I suggested. "The taxi driver is probably gone by now. Let's go back the way we came, and go out through the restaurant."

Eddie pushed his dark hair back off his forehead. "Good idea," he muttered.

We turned and started the long walk back. It was easy to keep in the right direction. We followed the hallways and made left turns instead of rights.

We walked quickly without speaking.

As we walked, I tried to remember our last name. Tried to remember Mum and Dad. Tried to picture their faces.

Tried to remember *something* about them.

Losing your memory is so terrifying. Much more frightening than being chased by someone.

That's because the problem is inside you. Inside your own mind.

You can't run away from it. You can't hide from it. And you can't solve it.

You just feel so helpless.

My only hope was that Mum and Dad would be waiting in the room. And that they could explain to Eddie and me what had happened to our memories.

"Oh, no!" Eddie cried, startling me from my thoughts.

We had reached the end of the final hallway. The hotel restaurant should be on the other side of the curtained glass door.

But there was no door.

No door back to the restaurant. No door at all Eddie and I were staring at a solid wall.

"No!" Eddie wailed. "Let us out! Let us out of here!" He pounded furiously on the wall with his fist.

I tugged him away. "This must be the wrong hallway," I told him. "We made a wrong turn."

"No!" he protested. "It's the right hallway! I know it is!"

"Then where is the restaurant?" I replied. "They didn't seal it up while we were walking the halls just now."

He stared up at me, his chin trembling, his dark eyes frightened. "Can't we go outside and walk around to the front?" he asked wearily.

"We could," I replied thoughtfully. "If we could find a door that led to the outside. But so far—"

I stopped when I heard voices.

I turned and saw a narrow hallway leading off to our right. The voices seemed to be floating through this hall I hadn't noticed before. Voices and laughter.

"That must be the restaurant down there," I told Eddie. "See? We just had one more turn to make. We'll be out of here in a few seconds."

His face brightened a little.

The voices and laughter grew louder as we made our way down the narrow corridor. Bright yellow light shone out from an open doorway at the end.

As we stepped into the doorway, we both cried out in surprise.

This was not the hotel restaurant we had our tea in.

I grabbed Eddie's arm as I stared in shock around the enormous room. Two blazing fireplaces provided the only light. People in strange costumes sat on low benches around long, wooden tables.

A whole deer or an elk was turning on a spit, roasting over a fire in the centre of the floor.

The tables were piled high with food—meats, whole cabbages, green vegetables, fruits, whole potatoes, and foods I didn't recognize.

I didn't see any plates or serving platters. The food was just strewn over the long tables. People reached in and pulled out what they wanted.

They ate noisily, talking loudly, laughing and singing, taking long drinks from metal wine cups, slapping the cups on the table-top and toasting each other merrily.

"They're all eating with their *hands*!" Eddie exclaimed.

He was right. I didn't see any silverware at the tables.

Two chickens, squawking loudly, fluttered across the floor, chased by a large brown dog. A woman had two babies in her lap. She ignored them while she chewed on a large hunk of meat.

"It's a fancy-dress party," I whispered to Eddie. We hadn't the nerve to move from the doorway. "This must be where those guys in the hoods were going."

I gazed in amazement at the colourful costumes in the room. Long robes, loose-fitting pyjama-type outfits of blue and green, leather waistcoats worn over black tights. A lot of men and women wore animal furs around their shoulders—despite the blazing heat from the fireplaces.

In one corner, a man appeared to be wearing an entire bearskin. He stood beside a giant wooden barrel, working a tap, filling metal cups with a thick, brown liquid that oozed from the barrel.

Two children in rags played tag under one of the long tables. Another child, dressed in green tights, chased after one of the squawking chickens.

"What a party!" Eddie whispered. "Who *are* these people?"

I shrugged. "I don't know. I can't understand what they're saying too well. Can you?"

Eddie shook his head. "Their accents are too weird."

"But maybe someone in here can tell us how to get outside," I suggested.

"Let's try," Eddie pleaded.

I led the way into the room. Even though I was walking slowly, timidly, I nearly tripped over a sleeping hound dog.

Eddie followed close behind as I made my way up to one of the men turning the roasting deer on the spit. He wore only knee breeches of some rough brown cloth. His forehead and the top of his body glistened with sweat.

"Excuse me, sir," I said.

He glanced up at me and his eyes bulged wide in surprise.

"Excuse me," I repeated. "Can you tell us how to get out of the hotel?"

He stared at me without replying, stared as if he had never seen a twelve-year-old girl in jeans and a T-shirt before.

Two little girls, wearing grey dresses down to the floor, walked up to Eddie and me, staring up at us with the same shocked expression as the man. Their streaky blonde hair fell wild and tangled behind their backs. It looked as if it had never been brushed in their lives!

They pointed at us and giggled.

And I suddenly realized that the entire room had grown silent.

As if someone had turned a knob and clicked off the sound.

My heart started to pound. The strong smell of the roasting deer choked my nostrils.

I turned to find everyone in the room gaping in open-mouthed wonder. Staring in silence at Eddie and me.

"I—I'm sorry to interrupt the party," I stammered in a tiny, frightened voice.

I let out a cry of surprise as they all climbed noisily to their feet. Food toppled off the table. One of the long benches clattered to the floor.

More children pointed and giggled.

Even the chickens seemed to stop clucking and strutting.

And then an enormous red-faced man in a long white gown raised his hand and pointed at Eddie and me. *"It's THEM!"* he bellowed. *"It's THEM!"*

"Do they *know* us?" Eddie whispered to me.

We stared back at them. Everyone seemed to freeze in place. The man stopped turning the deer on the spit. The only sound in the huge dining hall was the crackle of the fires in the twin fireplaces.

The man in the white gown slowly lowered his hand. His face darkened to a bright scarlet as he gaped at us in amazement.

"We just want to find the way out," I said. My voice sounded tiny and shrill.

No one moved. No one replied.

I took a deep breath and tried one more time. "Can anyone help us?"

Silence.

Who are these strange people? I wondered. *Why are they staring at us like that? Why won't they answer us?*

Eddie and I took a step back as they began to move towards us. Some of them were whispering excitedly, muttering to each other, gesturing with their hands.

"Eddie—we'd better get out of here!" I whispered.

I couldn't hear what they were saying. But I didn't like the excited expressions on their faces.

And I didn't like the way they were moving along the wall, moving to get behind us, to surround us.

"Eddie—run!" I screamed.

Angry cries rang out as we both spun around and hurtled towards the open doorway. Dogs barked. Children started to cry.

We darted back into the dark hallway and kept running.

I could still feel the heat of the fire on my face as we ran, still smell the tangy aroma of the roasting deer.

Their excited, angry cries followed us through the long hall. Gasping for breath, I glanced back, expecting to see them chasing after us.

But the hall was empty.

We turned a corner and kept going. Candles flickered on both sides of us. The floorboards groaned under our shoes.

The eerie, dim light. The voices far behind us. The endless tunnel of a hallway. All made me feel as if I were running through a dream.

We turned another corner and kept running.

The misty candlelight blurred as I ran. I'm floating through a dark orange cloud, I thought.

Do these empty, candlelit halls ever end?

Eddie and I both cried out happily as a door appeared in front of us.

A door we had never seen before.

It *has* to lead to the outside! I told myself.

We raced to the door. We didn't slow down as we reached it.

I stuck out both hands. Pushed hard.

The door flew open.

And we stepped out into bright sunlight.

Outside! We had escaped from the dark maze of the hotel corridors!

It took a few seconds for the harsh white glare to fade from my eyes.

I blinked several times. Then I gazed up and down the street.

"Oh, no!" I wailed, grabbing my brother's arm. "No! Eddie—what has *happened*?"

"It—it's daytime!" Eddie stammered.

But the bright sunlight wasn't the only shock. *Everything* had changed.

I felt as if I were watching a movie, and the scene had changed. And suddenly it was the next day—or the next week—and I was seeing an entirely different place.

I knew that only a few seconds had passed since Eddie and I had burst out of the hotel. But in that time, *everything* had changed.

We huddled close together and stared in one direction and then the next. We saw no cars. No buses. The street had vanished, replaced by a lumpy dirt road.

The tall buildings had disappeared, too. The road was dotted with small, white cottages with flat roofs and low, wooden shacks built without doors or windows.

A tall mound of straw stood beside the nearest cottage. Chickens clucked and strutted across the road or stood in front of cottages pecking in the dirt. A brown cow poked its head out from behind the mound of straw.

"What's going on?" Eddie asked. "Where *are* we?"

"It's like we stepped back in time," I said in a hushed voice. "Eddie—look at the people."

Two men walked by carrying lines of slender, silvery fish. The men had thick beards and wild, unbrushed hair. They wore loose-fitting grey smocks that dragged along the ground.

Two women in long, brown dresses were on their knees, pulling up root-type vegetables with their hands. A man leading a scrawny horse, its bones sticking out at its rib cage, stopped to say something to the two women.

"They look a lot like the people in the hotel," I told Eddie.

Thinking about the hotel made me turn around. "Oh, no!" I grabbed Eddie and made him turn around.

The hotel was gone.

In its place stood a long, low building built of brown stone. It appeared to be some sort of inn or meeting hall.

"I don't understand this," Eddie moaned. In the bright sunlight, he looked very pale. He scratched his dark brown hair. "Sue, we've got to get back to the hotel. I—I'm very mixed up."

"Me, too," I confessed.

219

I took a few steps along the dirt road. It must have rained recently. The road was soft and muddy.

I could hear cows mooing nearby.

This is central London! I told myself. How can I hear cows in central London? Where are all the tall buildings? The cars and taxis and double-decker buses?

I heard someone whistling. A blond-haired boy, dressed in an outfit made of black and brown rags, appeared from behind the long building. He carried a bundle of sticks in his arms.

He seemed about my age. My shoes sank into the mud as I hurried across the road to him. "Hey—!" I called. "Hi!"

He peered over the bundle of sticks at me. His blue eyes widened in surprise. His hair was long and unbrushed. It fluttered over his shoulders in the breeze. "Good day to you, miss," he said. His accent was so strange, I could barely understand him.

"Good day," I replied uncertainly.

"Are ye a traveller?" the boy asked, shifting the bundle on to his shoulder.

"Yes," I replied. "But my brother and I are lost. We can't find our hotel."

He narrowed his blue eyes at me. He appeared to be thinking hard.

"Our hotel," I repeated. "Can you tell us where it is? The Barclay?"

"Barclay?" he repeated the word. "Hotel?"

"Yes," I said. I waited for him to reply. But he just stared back at me, squinting his blue eyes and frowning.

"I do not know those foreign words," he said finally.

"Hotel?" I cried impatiently. "You know. A place where travellers stay?"

"Many stay at the abbey," he replied. He pointed to the long, low building behind us.

"No. I mean—" I started. I could see that he didn't understand me at all.

"I must be getting the wood along home," the boy said. He nodded goodbye, lowered the bundle from his shoulder, and headed down the road.

"Eddie, that boy—"I said. "He doesn't know what a hotel is! Do you believe—?"

I turned back. "Eddie?"

Eddie was gone.

"Eddie? Eddie?"

My voice grew higher and more frightened as I called his name.

Where did he go?

"Hey—Eddie!" I shouted.

The two women glanced up from their vegetable picking.

"Did you see where my brother went?" I called to them.

They shook their heads and returned to their work.

"Oh!" I had to jump out of the road as a cart, pulled by a groaning, grunting ox, came barrelling past. The driver, a fat, bare-chested man, his pouchy skin darkened by the sun, slapped the ropes that served as reins. He bellowed at the ox to move faster.

As the wagon rolled past, its wooden wheels sank into the mud, leaving deep ridges in the road. Chickens clucked and scurried out

222

of the way. The two women didn't even glance up.

I made my way to the entrance of the abbey. "Eddie? Are you back here?"

I pulled open the door and peered inside. The long candlelit hall stretched before me. I could see men in hooded robes gathered at a doorway.

We just came from there, I told myself as I closed the door. Eddie wouldn't go back inside.

So where was he?

How could he run off and leave me here? How could he just disappear like that?

I called his name a few more times. Then my throat tightened up. My mouth felt dry as cotton. "Eddie?" I called weakly.

My legs began to tremble as I walked to the side of the first cottage. *Don't panic, Sue*, I told myself. You'll find him. Just don't panic.

Too late.

I was really scared.

Eddie wouldn't suddenly wander off and go exploring without me. He was too scared.

So where was he?

I peered into the open doorway of the cottage. A sour smell floated out from inside. I could see a crude wooden table and a couple of wooden stools. No one in there.

I made my way behind the cottage. A grassy pasture stretched up a gently sloping hill. Four or five cows stood halfway up the hill, their heads lowered as they chewed the grass.

I cupped my hands around my mouth and called to my brother.

My only reply was the soft mooing of a cow.

With a worried sigh, I turned around and made my way back to the road. I guess I'll have to search every cottage, I decided. Eddie couldn't have gone very far.

I had only taken a few steps towards the next cottage when a shadow slid over the road.

Startled, I raised my eyes—and stared at the dark figure blocking my path.

His black cape fluttered behind him in the wind. He wore a new black hat, and his pale, pale face poked out from its dark brim.

I stepped back, out of his shadow. I raised my hands to my cheeks and stared at him in horrified silence.

"I said it was time for us to go," he said softly, moving closer.

"Wh-where is Eddie?" I managed to choke out. "Do you know where Eddie is?"

A thin-lipped smile crossed his pale face. "Eddie?" He sniggered. For some reason, my question seemed to amuse him. "Do not worry about *Eddie*," he replied with a sneer.

He took another step forward. His shadow fell over me again.

It made me shiver.

Glancing around, I saw that the two women picking vegetables had disappeared into their cottages. Everyone had disappeared. The road stood empty except for some chickens and a hound dog, asleep on its side in front of the straw pile.

225

"I—I don't understand," I stammered. "Who are you? Why are you chasing us? Where *are* we?"

My frantic questions only made him chuckle. "You know me," he replied softly.

"No!" I protested. "I don't know you! What is happening?"

"Your questions cannot delay your fate," he replied.

I stared hard at him, trying to study his face, searching for answers. But he lowered the brim of the black hat, hiding his eyes from view.

"You've made a mistake!" I cried. "You've got the wrong girl! I don't know you! I don't know anything!"

His smile faded. He shook his head. "Come with me now," he said firmly.

"No!" I shrieked. "Not until you tell me who you are! Not until you tell me where my brother is."

Brushing his heavy cape back, he took another step towards me. His boots sank heavily into the mud as he strode forwards.

"I won't come with you!" I screamed. My hands were still pressed hard against my cheeks. My legs were shaking so much, I nearly sank to the ground.

I glanced around, getting ready to run.

Would my trembling legs carry me?

"Do not think of running away," he said, as if reading my mind.

"But—but—" I spluttered.

"You will come with me now. It is time," he said.

He strode forward quickly, raised his gloved hands, and grabbed me by both shoulders.

I had no time to struggle. No time to try to break free.

The ground started to rumble.

I heard a groaning sound. A heavy slapping sound.

Another ox-cart bounced around the corner. I saw the driver slap the ox with a long rope.

The cart moved so fast. A blur of groaning animal and grinding wheels.

The black-caped man released his grasp and leaped back as the cart rolled at us.

I saw his black hat fly off. Saw him stumble in the deep rut in the mud at the side of the road. Saw him stagger back off-balance.

It was all the time I needed. I wheeled around and started to run. I bent low as I ran, hiding beside the grunting, straining ox. Then I turned sharply and dived between two small cottages.

I caught a glimpse of the black-caped man as I darted past the cottages. He was bending to pick up his hat. His bald head shone like an egg in the sunlight. He had no hair at all.

I was panting rapidly. My chest ached, and the blood throbbed at my temples.

Keeping low, I ran along the backs of the cottages. The green pasture stretched to my left. Nowhere to hide there.

The cottages grew closer together. I heard crying children. A woman was roasting some kind of blood-red sausage over a fire. She called out to me as I ran past. But I didn't slow down to reply.

Two scrawny black hounds came yapping after me, snapping at my legs. "Shoo!" I cried. "Shoo! Go home!"

Glancing back, I could see the tall, dark figure gliding easily over the grass, his cape sweeping up behind him.

He's catching up, I realized.

I have to find a hiding place, I told myself. Now!

I ducked between two small shacks—and nearly ran into a large, red-haired woman carrying a baby. The baby was swaddled in a heavy, grey blanket. Startled, the woman squeezed the baby to her chest.

"You've got to hide me!" I cried breathlessly.

"Go away from here!" the woman replied. She seemed more frightened than unfriendly.

"Please!" I begged. "He's chasing me!" I pointed through the space between the cottages.

We could both see the black-caped man running closer.

"Please! Don't let him catch me!" I pleaded. "Hide me! Hide me!"

The woman had her eyes on the black-caped man. She turned to me and shrugged her broad shoulders. "I cannot," she said.

I let out a long sigh, a sigh of defeat. I knew I couldn't run any further.

I knew the caped man would capture me easily.

The woman pressed the baby against the front of her black dress and turned to watch the man run towards us.

"I—I'll *pay* you!" I blurted out.

I suddenly remembered the coins in my pocket. The coins the taxi driver refused to take.

Would the woman take them now?

I shoved my hand into my pocket and pulled out the coins. "Here!" I cried. "Take them! Take them all! Just hide me—please!"

I jammed the coins into the woman's free hand.

As she raised her hand to examine them, her eyes bulged and her mouth dropped open.

She isn't going to take them, either, I thought.

She's going to throw them back at me as the taxi driver did.

But I was wrong.

"Gold sovereigns!" she exclaimed in a hushed voice. "Gold sovereigns. I saw one once when I was a little lass."

"Will you take them? Will you hide me?" I pleaded.

She dropped the coins into her dress. Then she shoved me through the open doorway of her little cottage.

It smelled of fish inside. I saw three beds on the floor beside a bare hearth.

"Quick—into the kindling basket," the woman instructed. "It's empty." She pushed me again, towards a large straw box with a lid.

My heart pounding, I pushed up the lid and scrambled inside. The lid dropped back down, covering me in darkness.

On my hands and knees, I crouched on the rough straw bottom of the box. I struggled to stop panting, to stop my heart from thudding in my chest.

The woman had taken the coins gladly, I realized. She didn't think they were play money, as the taxi driver had said.

The coins are very old, I decided.

And then a chill ran down my trembling body. I suddenly knew why everything looked so different—so old. We really have gone back in time, I told myself.

We are back in London hundreds of years ago. The caped man brought us back here with those white stones. He thinks I am someone else. He has been chasing me because he has mistaken me for someone else.

How do I make him see the truth? I wondered.

And how do I get out of the past, back to my real time?

I forced the questions from my mind—and listened.

I could hear voices outside the cottage. The woman's voice. And then the booming, deep voice of the black-caped man.

I held my breath so I could hear their words over the loud beating of my heart.

"She is right in here, sire," the woman said. I heard footsteps. And then their voices became louder. Closer. They were standing beside my basket.

"Where is she?" the caped man demanded.

"I put her in this box for you, sire," the woman replied. "She's all wrapped up for you. Ready for you to take her away."

My heart jumped to my throat. In the blackness of the box, I suddenly saw red.

That woman took my money, I thought angrily. And then she gave away my hiding place.

How could she do that to me?

I was still crouched on my hands and knees. So angry. So terrified. My entire body went numb, and I felt as if I would crumple to the basket floor in a heap.

Taking a deep breath, I twisted around and tried to push open the straw lid.

I let out a disappointed groan when it didn't budge.

Was it clasped shut? Or was the caped man holding it down?

It didn't matter. I was helpless. Trapped. I was his prisoner now.

The basket suddenly moved, knocking me against its side. I could feel it sliding over the floor of the cottage.

"Hey—!" I cried out. But my voice was muffled in the tiny box. I lowered myself to the rough straw floor, my heart pounding. "Let me out!"

The basket bounced again. Then I felt it slide some more.

"Lass! You—lass!" I lifted my head as I heard the woman whispering to me.

"I am so sorry," she said. "I hope you will find it in your heart to forgive me. But I dare not go against the Lord High Executioner."

"What?" I cried. "What did you say?"

The basket slid faster. Bumped hard. Bumped again.

"What did you say?" I repeated frantically.

Silence now.

I did not hear her voice again.

A moment later, I heard the whinny of horses. I was tossed against one side, then the other, as the basket was lifted up.

Soon after, the basket began to bounce and shake. And I heard the steady *clip-clop* of horses' hooves.

A helpless prisoner inside the straw basket, I knew I was on some kind of carriage or horse cart.

The Lord High Executioner?

Is that what the woman had said?

The shadowy man in the black cape and black hat—he is the Lord High Executioner?

Inside my tiny, dark prison, I began to shudder. I could not stop the chills that rolled down my back until my entire body felt cold and numb and tingly.

The Lord High Executioner.

The words kept repeating in my mind. Like a terrifying chant.

The Lord High Executioner.

And then I asked myself: *What does he want with me?*

27

The wagon stopped with a jolt. Then, a minute or so later, started up again.

Bouncing around inside the basket, I lost all track of time.

Where is he taking me? I wondered. *What does he plan to do?*

And: *Why me?*

My head hit the front of the basket as we jolted to another stop. I shivered. My body was drenched in a cold sweat.

The air in the box had become sour. I began gasping for fresh air.

I let out a cry as the lid suddenly flew open. The harsh sunlight made me shield my eyes.

"Remove her!" I heard the booming voice of the Executioner.

Strong arms grabbed me roughly and tugged me from the straw box. As my eyes adjusted to the light, I saw that I was being lifted by two grey-uniformed soldiers.

They set me on my feet. But my legs gave way, and I crumpled to the dirt.

"Stand her up," the Executioner ordered. I gazed up into the sun at him. His face was hidden once again in the shadow of his dark hat.

The soldiers bent to pick me up. Both of my legs had fallen asleep. My back ached from being tossed and tumbled in the cramped box.

"Let me go!" I managed to cry. "Why are you doing this?"

The Executioner didn't reply.

The soldiers held on to me until I could stand on my own.

"You've made a terrible mistake!" I told him, my voice trembling with anger, with fear. "I don't know why I am here or how I got here! But I am the wrong girl! I am not who you think I am!"

Again, he did not reply. He gave a signal with one hand, and the guards took my arms and turned me around.

And as I turned away from the Executioner, away from the sun, the dark castle rose in front of me. I saw the wall, the courtyard, the dark, slender towers looming up over the stone castle.

The Terror Tower!

He had brought me to the Terror Tower.

This is where Eddie and I had seen him for the

first time. This is where the Executioner had first chased after us.

In the twentieth century. In my time. In the time where I belonged. Hundreds of years in the future.

Somehow Eddie and I had been dragged back into the past, to a time where we didn't belong. And now Eddie was lost. And I was being led to the Terror Tower.

The Executioner led the way. The soldiers gripped my arms firmly, pulling me through the courtyard towards the castle entrance.

The courtyard was jammed with silent, grim-looking people. Dressed in rags and tattered, stained gowns, they stared at me as I was dragged past.

Some of them stood hunched like scarecrows, their eyes vacant, their faces blank, as if their minds were somewhere else. Some sat and wept, or stared at the sky.

A bare-chested old man sat under a tree frantically scratching his greasy tangles of white hair with both hands. A young man pressed a filthy rag against a deep cut in his dirt-caked foot.

Babies cried and wailed. Men and women sat in the dirt, moaning and muttering to themselves.

These sad, filthy people were all prisoners, I realized. I remembered our tour guide, Mr

Starkes, telling us that the castle had first been a fort, then a prison.

I shook my head sadly, wishing I were back on the tour. In the future, in the time where I belonged.

I didn't have long to think about the prisoners. I was shoved into the darkness of the castle. Dragged up the twisting stone steps.

The air felt wet and cold as I climbed. A heavy chill seemed to rise up the stairs with me.

"Let me go!" I screamed. "Please—let me go!"

The soldiers shoved me against the stone wall when I tried to pull free.

I cried out helplessly and tried again to tug myself loose. But they were too big, too strong.

The stone stairs curved round and round. We passed the cell on the narrow landing. Glancing towards it, I saw that it was jammed with prisoners. They stood in silence against the bars, their faces yellow and expressionless. Many of them didn't even look up as I passed.

Up to the steep, slippery stairs.

Up to the dark door at the top of the tower.

"No—please!" I begged. "This is all wrong! All wrong!"

But they slid the heavy metal bolt on the door and pulled the door open.

A hard shove from behind sent me sprawling into the tiny tower room. I stumbled to the floor, landing on my elbows and knees.

I heard the heavy door slam behind me. Then I heard the bolt sliding back into place.

Locked in.

I was locked in the tiny cell at the top of the Terror Tower.

"Sue!" A familiar voice called my name.

I raised myself to my knees. Glanced up. "Eddie!" I cried happily. "Eddie—how did you get here?"

My little brother had been sitting on the floor against the wall. Now he scrambled over to me and helped me to my feet. "Are you okay?" he asked.

I nodded. "Are *you* okay?"

"I guess so," he replied. He had a long dirt smear down one side of his face. His dark hair was matted wetly against his forehead. His eyes were red-rimmed and frightened.

"The caped man grabbed me," Eddie said. "Back in the town. In the street. You know. When that ox-cart came by."

I nodded. "I turned around, and you were gone."

"I tried to call to you," Eddie replied. "But the caped man covered my mouth. He handed me to his soldiers. And they pulled me behind one of the cottages."

"This is so awful!" I cried, struggling to hold my tears back.

"One of the soldiers lifted me on to his horse,"

240

Eddie said. "I tried to squirm away. But I couldn't. He brought me to the castle and dragged me up to the Tower."

"The caped man—he's the Lord High Executioner," I told my brother. "That's what I heard a woman call him."

The words made my brother gasp. His dark eyes locked on to mine. "Executioner?"

I nodded grimly.

"But why does he want *us*?" Eddie demanded. "Why has he been chasing *us*? Why are we locked up in this horrible tower?"

A sob escaped my throat. "I—I don't know," I stammered.

I started to say something else—but stopped when I heard noises outside the door.

Eddie and I huddled together in the centre of the room.

I heard the bolt slide open.

The door slowly began to open.

Someone was coming for us.

241

A white-haired man stepped into the room. His hair was wild and long, and fell in thick tangles behind his shoulders. He had a short white beard that ended in a sharp point.

He wore a purple robe that flowed down to the floor. His eyes were as purple as his robe. They squinted first at Eddie, then lingered on me.

"You have returned," he said solemnly. His voice was smooth and low. His purple eyes suddenly revealed sadness.

"Who are you?" I cried. "Why have you locked us in this tower?"

"Let us out!" Eddie demanded shrilly. "Let us out of here—right now!"

The long purple robe swept over the floor as the white-haired man moved towards us. He shook his head sadly, but didn't reply.

The cries and moans of prisoners down below floated into the tower room through the tiny window above our heads. Grey evening light spilled over us.

"You do not remember me," the man said softly.

"Of course not!" Eddie cried. "We don't belong here!"

"You've made a bad mistake," I told him.

"You do not remember me," he repeated, rubbing his pointed beard with one hand. "But you will."

He seemed gentle. Kind. Not at all like the Executioner.

But as his strange purple eyes locked on mine, I felt a shiver of fear. This man was powerful, I realized. This man was dangerous.

"Just let us go!" Eddie pleaded again.

The man sighed. "I wish it were in my power to release you, Edward," he said softly. "I wish it were in my power to release you, too, Susannah."

"Wait a minute." I held up a hand to signal *stop*. "Just wait a minute. My name is Sue. Not Susannah."

The old man's hands disappeared into the deep pockets of his robe. "Perhaps I should introduce myself," he said. "My name is Morgred. I am the king's sorcerer."

"You do magic tricks?" Eddie blurted out.

"Tricks?" The old man seemed confused by Eddie's question.

"Did you order us to be locked up in here?" I

asked him. "Did you have us brought back in time? Why? Why have you done this?"

"It isn't an easy story to tell, Susannah," Morgred replied. "You and Edward have to believe—"

"Stop calling me Susannah!" I shouted.

"I'm not Edward!" my brother insisted. "I'm Eddie. Everyone calls me Eddie."

The old man removed his hands from his robe pockets. He placed one hand on Eddie's shoulder, and one on mine.

"I had better start with the biggest surprise of all," he told us. "You are not Eddie and Sue. And you do not live in the twentieth century."

"Huh? What are you *saying*?" I cried.

"You really are Edward and Susannah," Morgred replied. "You are the Prince and Princess of York. And you have been ordered to the Tower by your uncle, the king."

"You're wrong!" Eddie cried. "We know who we are. You've made a big mistake!"

I suddenly felt cold all over. Morgred's words echoed in my ears. "You are not Eddie and Sue. You really are Edward and Susannah."

I took a step back, out from under his hand. I studied his face. Was he joking? Was he crazy?

His eyes revealed only sadness. His expression remained solemn, too solemn to be joking.

"I do not expect you to believe me," Morgred said, returning his hands to his robe pockets. "But my words are true. I cast a spell upon you. I tried to help you escape."

"Escape?" I cried. "You mean—escape from this tower?"

Morgred nodded. "I tried to help you escape your fate."

And as he said this, the voice of Mr Starkes,

the tour guide, returned to my ears. And I remembered the story he had told. I remembered the fate of Prince Edward and Princess Susannah.

The king's orders were to smother them.

Smothered with pillows.

"But we're not them!" I wailed. "You're just confused. Maybe Eddie and I look like them. Maybe we look a *lot* like them. But we're not the prince and princess. We're two kids from the twentieth century."

Morgred shook his head solemnly. "I cast a spell," he explained. "I erased your memories. You were locked in this tower. I wanted you to escape. First I whisked you away to the safety of the abbey, then I sent you as far into the future as I could."

"It's not true!" Eddie insisted, shrieking the words. "It's not true! Not true! I'm Eddie—not Edward. My name is Eddie!"

Morgred sighed again. "Just Eddie?" he asked, keeping his voice low and soft. "What is your full name, Eddie?"

"I—uh—well . . ." my brother stammered.

Eddie and I don't know our last name, I realized. And we don't know where we live.

"When I sent for you far into the future, I gave you new memories," Morgred said. "I gave you new memories so you could survive in new and distant time. But the memories were not complete."

"That's why we couldn't remember our parents!" I exclaimed to Eddie.

"But our parents—?" I started.

"Your parents, the rightful king and queen, are dead," Morgred told us. "Your uncle has named himself king. And he has ordered you to the Tower to get you out of the way."

"He—he's going to have us *murdered*!" I stammered.

Morgred nodded, shutting his eyes. "Yes. I am afraid he is. His men will be here soon. There is no way I can stop him now."

"I don't believe this," Eddie murmured. "I really don't."

But I could see the sadness in Morgred's purple eyes and hear it in his low, soft voice. The sorcerer was telling the truth.

The horror of the truth was sinking in. My brother and I weren't Eddie and Sue from the twentieth century. We lived in this dark and dangerous time. We were Edward and Susannah of York.

"I tried to send you as far from this Tower as possible," Morgred tried to explain again. "I sent you far into the future to start new lives. I wanted you to live there and never return. Never return to face doom in this castle."

"But what happened?" I demanded. "Why, then, are we back here, Morgred?"

"The Lord High Executioner was spying on me," Morgred explained, lowering his voice to a whisper. "He must have known that I wanted to help you escape. And, so—"

He stopped and tilted his head towards the door.

Was that a footstep? Was someone out there?

All three of us listened.

Silence now.

Morgred continued his story in a whisper. "When I cast the spell that sent you into the future, the Executioner must have hidden nearby. I used three white stones to cast the spell. Later, he stole the stones and performed the spell himself. He sent himself to the future to bring you back. And as you both know, he caught you and dragged you back here."

Morgred took a step forward. He raised his hand and placed it on my forehead.

The hand felt cold at first. Then it grew warmer and warmer, until I pulled away from the blazing heat.

As I pulled back, my memory returned.

Once again, I became Princess Susannah of York. My true identity. I remembered my parents, the king and queen. And all my memories of growing up in the royal castle returned.

My brother glared angrily at Morgred. "What did you do to my sister?" he cried, backing up until he bumped into the stone wall.

Morgred placed his hand on my brother's

249

forehead. And I watched my brother's expression change as his memory returned and he realized he really was the prince.

"How did you do it, Morgred?" Edward asked, pushing his dark brown hair off his forehead. "How did you send Susannah and me to the future? Can you perform the spell again?"

"Yes!" I cried. "Can you perform it once more? Can you send us to the future now—before the king's men come?"

Morgred shook his head sadly. "Alas, I cannot," he murmured. "I do not have the three stones. As I told you, they were stolen by the Lord High Executioner."

A smile slowly spread over my brother's face. He reached into his pocket. "Here they are!" Eddie announced. He winked at me. "I stole them back again when the Executioner captured me in town."

Edward handed the stones to Morgred. "Fastest hands in all of Britannia!" he declared.

Morgred did not smile. "It is a simple spell, actually," the wizard said. He raised the three stones into the air, and they began to glow.

"I pile the stones up one on top of the other," Morgred explained. "I wait for them to glow with a bright white heat. Then I pronounce the words *'Movarum, Lovaris, Movarus.'* I then call out the year to which the traveller is to be sent."

"That's the whole spell?" Edward asked,

staring at the smooth, glowing stones in Morgred's hand.

Morgred nodded. "That is the spell, Prince Edward."

"Well, do it again! Please hurry!" I begged him. His expression grew even sadder. "I cannot," he said, his voice breaking with emotion.

He returned the three stones to the pocket of his robe. Then he uttered a long, unhappy sigh. "It is my fondest wish to help you children," he whispered. "But if I help you to escape again, the king will torture me and put me to a painful death. And then I will not be able to use my magic to help all the people of Britain."

Tears brimmed in his purple eyes and ran down his wrinkled cheeks. He gazed unhappily at my brother and me. "I—I only hope that you enjoyed your brief time in the future," he said in a whisper.

I shuddered. "You—you really cannot help us?" I pleaded.

"I cannot," he replied, lowering his eyes to the floor.

"Even if we *ordered* you?" Edward asked.

"Even if you ordered me," Morgred repeated. With an emotional cry, he wrapped Edward in a hug. Then he turned and hugged me, too. "I am helpless," he whispered. "I beg your forgiveness. But I am helpless."

"How long do we have to live?" I asked in a tiny, trembling voice.

"Perhaps a few hours," Morgred replied, avoiding my eyes. He turned away. He could not bear to face us.

A heavy silence fell over the tiny room. The grey light filtered down from the window above our heads. The air suddenly felt cold and damp.

I couldn't stop shivering.

Edward startled me by leaning close and whispering in my ear. "Susannah, look!" he whispered excitedly. "The door. Morgred left the door open when he entered."

I turned to the door. Edward was right. The heavy wooden door stood nearly half open.

We still have a chance, I thought, my heart beginning to race. We still have a tiny chance.

"Edward—*run*!" I screamed.

I took a running step.

And froze in mid-air.

I turned to see Edward freeze, too, his arms outstretched, his legs bent in a running position.

I struggled to move. But I couldn't. I felt as if my body had turned to stone.

It took me a few seconds to realize that Morgred had cast a spell on us. Frozen stiffly in the centre of the tiny room, I watched the sorcerer make his way to the door.

Halfway out, he turned back to us. "I'm so sorry," he said in a trembling voice. "But I cannot allow you to escape. Please understand. I did my best. I really did. But now I am helpless. Truly helpless."

Tears rolled down his cheeks, into his white beard. He gave us one last sad glance. Then the door slammed hard behind him.

As soon as the door was bolted from the

outside, the spell wore off. Edward and I could move again.

I sank to the floor. I suddenly felt weak. Weary.

Edward stood tensely beside me, his eyes on the door.

"What are we going to do?" I asked my brother. "Poor Morgred. He tried to help us. He wanted to help us again. But he couldn't. If only—"

I stopped talking when I heard the heavy footsteps outside the door.

At first, I thought it was Morgred returning.

But then I heard hushed voices. The sounds of more than one man.

Right outside the door now.

And I recognized the booming voice of one of them. The Lord High Executioner.

I climbed tensely to my feet and turned to Edward. "They've come for us," I whispered.

To my surprise, Edward's face remained calm.

He raised his hand. He had something hidden in his closed fist.

As he opened his fist, I recognized the three stones. Morgred's smooth, white stones.

They immediately began to glow.

"Edward—again?" I cried.

A smile crossed his lips. His dark eyes lit up excitedly. "I lifted them from Morgred's robe when he hugged me."

"Do you remember the spell?" I demanded.

Edward's smile faded. "I—I think so."

I could hear the Executioner outside the door. The heavy treading of boots on the stone stairs.

"Edward—please hurry!" I urged.

I heard the bolt slide outside the door.

I heard the heavy wooden door begin to slide open.

Edward struggled to stack the glowing stones

255

one on top of the other. The one on top kept slipping off.

Finally, he held all three in a small tower in his palm.

The door slid open a few inches more.

Edward held the glowing stones high. And called out the words, *"Movarum, Lovaris, Movarus!"*

The glowing stones exploded in a flash of white light.

The light faded quickly.

I glanced around.

"Oh, Edward!" I wailed in disappointment. "It didn't work! We're still in the Tower!"

Before my stunned brother could reply, the door swung all the way open.

And there they stood. A tour group.

I didn't recognize the tour leader. She was a young woman, dressed in layers of red and yellow T-shirts, and a short skirt over black tights.

I grinned at Edward. I felt so happy, I didn't think I would ever stop grinning!

"You did it, Edward!" I cried. "You did it! Your spell *did* work!"

"Call me Eddie," he replied, laughing glee-fully. "Call me Eddie, okay, *Sue*?"

The spell had worked perfectly. We were back in the twentieth century. Back in the Tower—as tourists!

"This tiny Tower room is where Prince Edward and Princess Susannah of York were held as prisoners," the tour guide announced. "They were held there and sentenced to death. But they were never executed."

"They didn't die up here?" I asked the tour

guide. "What happened?"

The tour guide shrugged. She chewed her gum harder. "No one knows. On the night they were to be murdered, the prince and princess vanished. Disappeared into thin air. It is a mystery that will never be solved."

Members of the tour group mumbled to each other, gazing around the small room.

"Look at the thick, stone walls," the tour guide continued, chewing her gum as she talked. "Look at the barred window so high above. How did they escape? We will never know."

"I guess *we* know the answer to the mystery," someone whispered behind me.

Eddie and I turned to see Morgred grinning at us. He winked. I saw that he was wearing a purple sports jacket and dark grey trousers.

"Thanks for bringing me along," he said happily.

"We had to bring you, Morgred," Eddie replied. "We need a parent."

Morgred raised a finger to his mouth. "Hush! Don't call me Morgred. I'm Mr Morgan now. Okay?"

"Okay," I said. "And I guess I'm Sue Morgan. And this is Eddie Morgan." I slapped my brother on the back.

The tour group started out of the Tower room, and we followed. Eddie pulled the three white stones from his jeans pocket and began juggling them.

"If I hadn't borrowed these from your robe," he told Mr Morgan, "that tour guide would be telling a very different story—wouldn't she!"

"Yes, she would," the sorcerer replied thoughtfully. "A very different story."

"Let's get out of here!" I cried. "I never want to see this tower again."

"I'm starving!" Eddie exclaimed.

I suddenly realized I was starving, too.

"Shall I perform a food spell?" Mr Morgan suggested.

Eddie and I each let out a load groan. "I think I've had enough spells to last a lifetime," I said. "How about we go to Burger Palace for some good old twentieth-century hamburgers and fries!"

The Cuckoo Clock
of Doom

"Michael, your shoe's untied."

My sister, Tara, sat on the front steps, grinning at me. Another one of her dumb jokes.

I'm not an idiot. I knew better than to look down at my shoe. If I did, she'd slap me under the chin or something.

"I'm not falling for that old trick," I told her.

Mum had just called me and the brat inside for dinner. An hour before she had made us go outside because she couldn't stand our fighting any more.

It was impossible not to fight with Tara.

When it comes to stupid tricks, Tara never knows when to quit. "I'm not kidding," she insisted. "Your shoe's untied. You're going to trip."

"Knock it off, Tara," I said. I started up the front steps.

My left shoe seemed to cling to the cement. I pulled it up with a jerk.

"Yuck!" I'd stepped on something sticky.

I glanced at Tara. She's a skinny little squirt, with a wide red mouth like a clown's and stringy brown hair that she wears in two pigtails.

Everyone says she looks exactly like me. I hate it when they say that. My brown hair is not stringy, for one thing. It's short and thick. And my mouth is normal-sized. No one has ever said I look like a clown.

I'm a little short for my age, but not skinny.

I do *not* look like Tara.

She was watching me, giggling. "You'd better look down," she taunted in her singsong voice.

I glanced down at my shoe. It wasn't untied, of course. But I'd just stepped on a huge wad of gum. If I had looked down to check my shoe-laces, I would have seen it.

But Tara knew I *wouldn't* look down. Not if she told me to.

Tricked by Tara the Terror again.

"You're going to get it, Tara," I grumbled. I tried to grab her, but she dodged out of reach and ran into the house.

I chased her into the kitchen. She screamed and hid behind my mother.

"Mum! Hide me! Michael's going to get me!" she shrieked.

As if she were afraid of me. Fat chance.

"Michael Webster!" Mum scolded. "Stop chasing your little sister."

She glanced at my feet and added, "Is that gum on your shoe? Oh, Michael, you're tracking it all over the floor!"

"Tara *made* me step on it!" I whined.

Mum frowned. "Do you expect me to believe that? Michael, you're fibbing again."

"I am not!" I cried.

Mum shook her head in disgust. "If you're going to tell a lie, Michael, at least make it a good one."

Tara peeked out from behind Mum and taunted me. "Yeah, *Michael*."

Then she laughed. She loved this.

She's always getting me into trouble. My parents always blame me for stuff that's *her* fault. But does Tara ever do anything wrong? Oh, *no*, never. She's a perfect angel. Not a bad bone in her body.

I'm twelve. Tara's seven. She's made the last seven years of my life miserable.

Too bad I don't remember the first five very well. The pre-Tara years. They must have been awesome! Quiet and peaceful—and fun!

I went out to the back porch and scraped the sticky gum off my shoe. I heard the doorbell ring and Dad calling, "It's here! I'll get it."

Inside, everybody gathered around the front door. Two men were struggling to carry something heavy into the house. Something long and narrow and wrapped with padded grey cloth.

"Careful," Dad warned them. "It's very old. Bring it in here."

Dad let the delivery guys into the den. They set the thing down on one end and began to unwrap it. It was about as wide as me and maybe thirty centimetres taller.

"What is it?" Tara asked.

Dad didn't answer right away. He rubbed his hands together in anticipation. Our cat, Bubba, slinked into the room and rubbed against Dad's legs.

The grey cloth fell away, and I saw a very fancy old clock. It was mostly black but painted with lots of silver, gold and blue designs, and decorated with scrolls, carvings, knobs and buttons.

The clock itself had a white face with gold hands and gold Roman numerals. I saw little secret doors hidden under the paint designs, and a big door in the middle of the clock.

The delivery guys gathered up the grey padding. Dad gave them some money, and they left.

"Isn't it great?" Dad gushed. "It's an antique cuckoo clock. It was a bargain. You know that shop opposite my office, Anthony's Antiques and Stuff?"

We all nodded.

"It's been in the shop for fifteen years," Dad told us, patting the clock. "Every time I pass

Anthony's, I stop and stare at it. I've always loved it. Anthony finally put it on sale."

"Cool," Tara said.

"But you've been bargaining with Anthony for years, and he always refused to lower the price," Mum said. "Why now?"

Dad's face lit up. "Well, today I went into the shop at lunchtime, and Anthony told me he'd discovered a tiny flaw on the clock. Something wrong with it."

I scanned the clock. "Where?"

"He wouldn't say. Do you see anything, kids?"

Tara and I began to search the clock for flaws. All the numbers on the face were correct, and both the hands were in place. I didn't see any chips or scratches.

"I don't see anything wrong with it," Tara said.

"Me, neither," I added.

"Neither do I," Dad agreed. "I don't know what Anthony's talking about. I told him I wanted to buy the clock anyway. He tried to talk me out of it, but I insisted. If the flaw is so tiny we don't even notice it, what difference does it make? Anyway, I really do love this thing."

Mum cleared her throat. "I don't know, dear. Do you think it really belongs in the den?" I could tell by her face that she didn't like the clock as much as Dad did.

"Where else could we put it?" Dad asked.

"Well—maybe the garage?"

Dad laughed. "I get it—you're joking!"

Mum shook her head. She wasn't joking. But she didn't say anything more.

"I think this clock is just what the den needs, honey," Dad added.

On the right side of the clock I saw a little dial. It had a gold face and looked like a miniature clock. But it had only one hand.

Tiny numbers were painted in black along the outside of the dial, starting at 1800 and ending at 2000. The thin gold hand pointed to one of the numbers: 1995.

The hand didn't move. Beneath the dial, a little gold button had been set into the wood.

"Don't touch that button, Michael," Dad warned. "This dial tells the current year. The button moves the hand to change the year."

"That's kind of silly," Mum said. "Who ever forgets what year it is?"

Dad ignored her. "See, the clock was built in 1800, where the dial starts. Every year the pointer moves one notch to show the date."

"So why does it stop at two thousand?" Tara asked.

Dad shrugged. "I don't know. I guess the clockmaker couldn't imagine the year two thousand would ever come. Or maybe he figured the clock wouldn't last that long."

"Maybe he thought the world would blow up in 1999," I suggested.

"Could be," Dad said. "Anyway, please don't touch the dial. In fact, I don't want anyone touching the clock at all. It's very old and very, very delicate. Okay?"

"Okay, Dad," Tara said.

"I won't touch it," I promised.

"Look," Mum said, pointing at the clock. "It's six o'clock. Dinner's almost—"

Mum was interrupted by a loud gong. A little door just over the clock face slid open—and a bird flew out. It had the meanest bird face I ever saw—and it dived for my head.

I screamed. "It's alive!"

Cuckoo! Cuckoo!

The bird flapped its yellow feathers. Its eerie, bright blue eyes glared at me. It squawked six times. Then it jumped back inside the clock. The little door slid shut.

"It's not alive, Michael," Dad said, laughing. "It sure is real-looking, though, isn't it? Wow!"

"You birdbrain!" Tara teased. "You were scared! Scared of a cuckoo clock!" She reached out and pinched me.

"Get off me," I growled. I shoved her away.

"Michael, don't push your sister," Mum said. "You don't realize how strong you are. You could hurt her."

"Yeah, Michael," Tara said.

Dad kept admiring the clock. He could hardly take his eyes off it. "I'm not surprised the cuckoo startled you," he said. "There's something special about this clock. It comes from the

270

Black Forest of Germany. It's supposed to be enchanted."

"Enchanted?" I echoed. "You mean, magic? How?"

"Legend has it that the man who built this clock had magical powers. He put a spell on the clock. They say if you know the secret, you can use the clock to go back in time."

Mum scoffed. "Did Anthony tell you that? What a great way to sell an old clock. Claim it has magic powers!"

Dad wouldn't let her spoil his fun. "You never know," he said. "It could be true. Why not?"

"I think it's true," Tara said.

"Herman, I wish you wouldn't tell the kids these wild stories," Mum chided. "It's not good for them. And it only encourages Michael. He's always making things up, telling fibs and impossible stories. I think he gets it from you."

I protested. "I don't make things up! I *always* tell the truth!"

How could Mum say that about me?

"I don't think it hurts the kids to use their imaginations once in a while," Dad said.

"Imagination is one thing," Mum said. "Lies and fibs are something else."

I fumed. Mum was so unfair to me. The worst part was the expression of victory on Tara's

271

face. Making me look bad was her mission in life. I wanted to wipe that smirk off her face for ever.

"Dinner's almost ready," Mum announced, leaving the den. The cat followed her. "Michael, Tara—go and wash your hands."

"And remember," Dad warned. "No one touches the clock."

"Okay, Dad," I said.

Dinner smelled good. I started for the bathroom to wash. As I passed Tara, she stomped hard on my foot.

"Ow!" I yelled.

"Michael!" Dad barked. "Stop making so much noise."

"But, Dad, Tara stomped on my foot."

"It couldn't have hurt that much, Michael. She's a lot smaller than you are."

My foot throbbed. I limped to the bathroom. Tara followed me.

"You're such a baby," she taunted.

"Be quiet, Tara," I said. How did I get the worst sister in the world?

We had pasta with broccoli and tomato sauce for dinner. Mum was on a big no-meat, low-fat kick. I didn't mind. Pasta was better than what we'd had the night before—lentil soup.

"You know, honey," Dad complained to Mum, "a hamburger now and then never hurt anybody."

"I disagree," Mum said. She didn't have to say more. We'd all heard her lectures about meat and fat and chemicals before.

Dad covered his pasta with a thick layer of Parmesan cheese.

"Maybe the den should be off limits for a while," Dad suggested. "I hate to think of you two playing in there and breaking the clock."

"But, Dad, I have to do my homework in the den tonight," I said. "I'm doing a report on 'Transportation in Many Lands'. And I need to use the encyclopaedia."

"Can't you take it up to your room?" Dad asked.

"The whole encyclopaedia?"

Dad sighed. "No, I guess you can't. Well, all right. You can use the den tonight."

"I need to use the encyclopaedia, too," Tara announced.

"You do not," I snapped. She wanted to hang around the den and bug me, that was all.

"I do, too. I'm supposed to read about the gold rush."

"You're making that up. You don't study the gold rush in the second grade. That's not until fourth."

"What do you know about it? Mrs Dolin is teaching us the gold rush *now*. Maybe I'm in a smarter class than you were."

Mum said, "Michael, really. If Tara says she needs to use the encyclopaedia, why start a fight about it?"

I sighed and stuffed a forkful of pasta in my mouth. Tara stuck her tongue out at me.

There's no point in talking, I thought. All it does is get me into trouble.

I lugged my backpack into the den after dinner. No sign of Tara—yet. Maybe I'd be able to get some homework done before she came in and started pestering me.

I dumped my books on Dad's desk. The clock caught my eye. It wasn't pretty—kind of ugly, really. But I liked looking at all those scrolls and buttons and knobs. It really did seem as if the clock could be magic.

I thought about the flaw Dad had mentioned. I wondered what it was. Some kind of bump? A missing notch on one of the gears? Maybe a piece of chipped paint?

I glanced back at the door to the den. Bubba wandered through it, purring. I petted him.

Mum and Dad were still in the kitchen, cleaning up after dinner. I didn't think it would matter if I just looked at the clock a little.

Careful not to touch any buttons, I stared at the dial that showed the year. I ran my fingers along a curve of silver at the edge of the clock. I glanced at the little door over the face of the clock. I knew the cuckoo sat behind the door, waiting to leap out at the right time.

I didn't want to be surprised by the bird again. I checked the time. Five minutes to eight.

Under the face of the clock I saw another door. A big door. I touched its gold knob.

What's behind this door? I wondered. Maybe the gears of the clock, or a pendulum.

I glanced over my shoulder again. No one was looking. No problem if I just peeked behind that big clock door.

I tugged on the gold knob. The door was stuck. I pulled harder.

The door flew open.

I let out a scream as an ugly green monster burst out of the clock. It grabbed me and knocked me to the floor.

"Mum! Dad! Help!" I shrieked.

The monster raised its long claws over me. I covered my face, waiting to be slashed.

"Goochy goochy goo!" The monster giggled and tickled me with its claws.

I opened my eyes. Tara! Tara in her old Halloween costume!

She rolled on the floor, giggling. "You're so easy to scare!" she shouted. "You should have seen your face when I jumped out of the clock!"

"It's not funny!" I cried. "It's—"

Gong.

Cuckoo, cuckoo, cuckoo, cuckoo!

The bird popped out of the clock and started cuckoo-ing. Okay, I admit it scared me again. But did Tara have to clutch her sides, laughing at me that way?

"What's going on in here?" Dad stood in the doorway, glaring down at us.

He pointed at the clock. "What's that door doing open? Michael, I *told* you to stay away from the clock!"

"ME?" I cried.

"He was trying to catch the cuckoo," Tara lied.

"I *thought* so," Dad said.

"Dad, that's not true! Tara's the one who—"

"Enough of that, Michael. I'm sick of hearing you blame Tara every time you do something wrong. Maybe your mother is right. Maybe I have been encouraging your imagination a little too much."

"That's not fair!" I yelled. "I don't have any imagination! I *never* make anything up!"

"Dad, he's lying," Tara said. "I came in here and saw him playing with the clock. I tried to stop him."

Dad nodded, swallowing every word his precious Tara said.

There was nothing I could do. I stormed off to my room and slammed the door.

Tara was the biggest pain in the world, and she never got blamed for anything. She even ruined my birthday.

I turned twelve three days ago. Usually, people like their birthday. It's supposed to be fun, right?

Not for me. Tara made sure my birthday was

277

the worst day of my life. Or at least *one* of the worst.

First, she ruined my present.

I could tell my parents were very excited about this present. My mother kept hopping around like a chicken, saying, "Don't go in the garage, Michael! Whatever you do, don't go in the garage!"

I knew she'd hidden my present in there. But just to torture her, I asked, "Why not? Why can't I go in the garage? The lock on my bedroom door is broken, and I need to borrow one of Dad's tools..."

"No, no!" Mum exclaimed. "Tell your father to fix the lock. He'll get the tools. You can't go in there, because... well... there's a huge mound of rubbish in there. It really stinks. It smells so bad, you could get sick from it!"

Sad, isn't it? And she thinks I get my "imagination" from Dad!

"All right, Mum," I promised. "I won't go in the garage."

And I didn't—even though the lock on my door really was broken. I didn't want to spoil whatever surprise they had cooked up.

They were throwing me a big birthday party that afternoon. A bunch of kids from school were coming over. Mum baked a cake and made snacks for the party. Dad ran around the house, setting up chairs and hanging crêpe paper.

"Dad, would you mind fixing the lock on my door?" I asked.

I like my privacy—and I *need* that lock. Tara had broken it a week earlier. She'd been trying to kickbox the door down.

"Sure, Michael," Dad agreed. "Anything you say. After all, you're the birthday boy."

"Thanks."

Dad took the toolbox upstairs and worked on the lock. Tara lounged around the dining room making trouble. As soon as Dad was gone, she pulled down a crêpe paper streamer and left it lying on the floor.

Dad fixed the lock and returned the tools to the garage. As he passed through the dining room, he noticed the torn-down streamer.

"Why won't this crêpe paper stay up?" he mumbled. He taped it back up. A few minutes later, Tara tore it down again.

"I know what you're doing, Tara," I told her. "Stop trying to wreck my birthday."

"I don't have to wreck it," she said. "It's bad all by itself—just because it's the day you were born." She pretended to shudder in horror.

I ignored her. It was my birthday. Nothing could keep me from having fun, not even Tara.

That's what I *thought*.

About half an hour before the party, Mum and Dad called me into the garage.

I pretended to go along with Mum's silly story. "What about the horrible rubbish?"

"Oh, that," Mum clucked. "I made it up."

"Really?" I said. "Wow. It was so believable."

"If you believed that, you must be a moron," Tara said.

Dad threw open the garage door. I stepped inside.

There stood a brand-new 21-speed bike. The bike I'd wanted for a long time.

The coolest bike I'd ever seen!

"Do you like it?" Mum asked.

"I love it!" I cried. "It's awesome! Thanks!"

"Cool bike, Mike," Tara said. "Mum, I want one of these for *my* birthday."

Before I could stop her, she climbed up on the seat of my new bike.

"Tara, get off!" I yelled.

She didn't listen. She tried to reach her feet to the pedals, but her legs were too short. The bike fell over.

"Tara!" Mum cried, running to the little brat's side. "Are you hurt?"

Tara stood up and brushed herself off. "I'm okay. I scraped my knee a little, though."

I picked up my bike and inspected it. It was no longer perfectly shiny and black. There was a huge white scratch across the middle bar.

It was practically ruined.

"Tara, you wrecked my bike!"

"Let's not get overexcited, Michael," Dad said. "It's only a scratch."

"Don't you even care about your sister?" Mum asked. "She could've been hurt!"

"It's her own fault! She shouldn't have touched my bike in the first place!"

"Michael, you have a lot to learn about being a good brother," Dad said.

They make me so mad sometimes!

"Let's go inside," Mum said. "Your friends will be here soon."

The party. I thought the party would make me feel better. After all, there would be cake, presents, and my best friends. What could go wrong?

It started out okay. One by one my friends arrived, and they all brought me presents. I'd invited five guys: David, Josh, Michael B., Henry and Lars; and three girls: Ceecee, Rosie and Mona.

I wasn't so crazy about Ceecee and Rosie, but I really liked Mona. She has long, shiny brown hair and a turned-up nose that's kind of cute. She's tall, and good at basketball. There's something sort of cool about her.

Ceecee and Rosie are Mona's best friends. I had to invite them if I was going to invite Mona. They always go everywhere together.

Ceecee, Rosie and Mona arrived all at once.

They took off their jackets. Mona was wearing pink dungarees over a white turtleneck. She looked great. I didn't care what the other girls were wearing.

"Happy birthday, Michael!" they all called out at the door.

"Thanks," I said.

They each handed me a gift. Mona's was small and flat and wrapped in silver paper. Probably a CD, I figured. But which one? What kind of CD would a girl like Mona think a guy like me would like?

I set the presents on top of the pile in the living room.

"Hey, Michael—what did your parents give you?" David asked.

"Just a bike," I said, trying to be cool about it. "A twenty-one speed."

I put on a CD. Mum and Tara brought in plates of sandwiches. Mum went back to the kitchen, but Tara stayed.

"Your little sister is so cute," Mona said.

"Not once you get to know her," I muttered.

"Michael! That's not very nice," Mona said.

"He's a terrible big brother," Tara told her. "He yells at me all the time."

"I do not! Get lost, Tara."

"I don't have to." She stuck her tongue out at me.

"Let her stay, Michael," Mona said. "She's not bothering anybody."

"Hey, Mona," Tara chirped. "You know, Michael really likes you."

Mona's eyes widened. "He does?"

My face got red-hot. I glared at Tara. I wanted to strangle her right then and there. But I couldn't—too many witnesses.

Mona started laughing. Ceecee and Rosie laughed, too. Luckily, the guys didn't hear this. They were around the CD player, skipping from cut to cut.

What could I say? I *did* like Mona. I couldn't deny it—it would hurt her feelings. But I couldn't admit it, either.

I wanted to die. I wanted to sink through the floor and die.

"Michael, your face is all red!" Mona cried.

Lars heard this and called out, "What did Webster do now?"

Some of the guys call me by my last name.

I grabbed Tara and dragged her into the kitchen, Mona's laughter ringing in my ears.

"Thanks a lot, Tara," I whispered. "Why did you have to tell Mona I like her?"

"It's true, isn't it?" the brat said. "I always tell the truth."

"Yeah, right!"

"Michael—" Mum interrupted. "Are you being mean to Tara again?"

I stormed out of the kitchen without answering her.

"Hey, Webster," Josh called when I returned to the living room. "Let's see your new bike."

Good, I thought. A way to get away from the girls.

I led them to the garage. They all stared at the bike and nodded at each other. They seemed really impressed. Then Henry grabbed the handlebars.

"Hey, what's this big scratch?" he said.

"I know," I explained. "My sister . . ."

I stopped and shook my head. What was the use?

"Let's go back and open my presents," I suggested.

We trooped back into the living room.

At least I've got more presents coming, I thought. Tara can't ruin those.

But Tara always find a way.

When I entered the living room, I found Tara sitting in the middle of a pile of torn-up wrapping paper. Rosie, Mona and Ceecee sat around her, watching.

Tara had opened all my presents for me.

Thanks so much, Tara.

She was ripping open the last present—Mona's.

"Look what Mona gave you, Michael!" Tara shouted.

It *was* a CD.

"I've heard there are some great *love* songs on it," Tara teased.

Everybody laughed. They all thought Tara was a riot.

Later, we all sat down in the dining room for cake and ice-cream. I carried the cake myself. Mum followed me, holding plates, candles, and matches.

It was my favourite kind of cake, chocolate-chocolate.

Balancing the cake in my hands, I stepped through the kitchen door and into the dining room.

I didn't see Tara pressed against the wall. I didn't see her stick her bratty little foot in the doorway.

I tripped. The cake flew out of my hands.

I landed on top of the cake. Face down. Of course.

Some kids gasped. Some tried to muffle their laughter.

I sat up and wiped the brown frosting from my eyes.

The first face I saw was Mona's. She was shaking with laughter.

Mum leaned over and scolded me. "What a mess! Michael, why don't you look where you're going?"

I listened to the laughter and stared at my ruined cake. I had no candles to blow out now. But it didn't matter. I decided to make a wish, anyway.

I wish I could start this birthday all over again.

I stood up, covered in gooey brown cake. My friends howled.

"You look like the Hulk!" Rosie cried.

Everybody laughed harder than ever.

They all had a great time at my party. Everyone did.

Except for me.

My birthday was bad—very bad. But ruining it wasn't the worst thing Tara did to me.

Nobody would believe the worst thing.

It happened the week before my birthday. Mona, Ceecee and Rosie were coming over. We all had parts in the school play, and planned to rehearse together at my house.

The play was a new version of *The Frog Prince*. Mona played the princess, and Ceecee and Rosie were her two silly sisters. Perfect casting, I thought.

I played the frog, before the princess kissed him and turns him into a prince. For some reason, our drama teacher didn't want me to play the prince. Josh got that part.

Anyway, I decided that the frog is a better part. Because Mona, the princess, kisses the *frog*, not the prince.

The girls would arrive any minute.

Tara sat on the rug in the den, torturing our cat, Bubba. Bubba hated Tara almost as much as I did.

Tara lifted Bubba by the hind legs, trying to

287

make him do a handstand. Bubba yowled and squirmed and wriggled away. But Tara caught him and made him do a handstand again.

"Stop that, Tara," I ordered.

"Why?" Tara said. "It's fun."

"You're hurting Bubba."

"No, I'm not. He likes it. See? He's smiling." She let go of his hind legs and grabbed him with one hand under his front legs. With the other hand she lifted the corners of his mouth and stretched them into a pained smile.

Bubba tried to bite her. He missed.

"Tara," I said, "let him go. And get out of here. My friends are coming over."

"No." Now Tara tried to make Bubba walk on his front paws. He fell and bumped his nose.

"Tara, stop it!" I cried. As I tried to take Bubba away from her, she let the cat go. Bubba meowed and scratched me across the arm.

"Ow!" I dropped Bubba. He ran away.

"Michael, what were you doing to that cat?" Mum stood in the doorway. Bubba slipped past her into the hall.

"Nothing! He scratched me!"

"Stop teasing him, and he won't scratch you," Mum scolded. She left, calling over her shoulder, "I'm going upstairs to lie down for a while. I have a headache."

The doorbell rang. "We'll get it, Mum!" I called.

I knew it must be the girls at the door. I wanted to surprise them in my frog costume, but I wasn't ready yet.

"Answer the door, Tara," I told the brat. "Tell Mona and the others to wait for me in the den. I'll be right back."

"Okay," Tara said. She trotted off to the front door. I hurried upstairs to change into my costume.

I pulled the costume out of my closet. I took off my trousers and shirt. I picked up the frog suit, trying to open the zipper. It was stuck.

I stood there in my underwear, tugging at the zipper. Then my bedroom door clicked open.

"Here he is, girls," I heard Tara say. "He told me to bring you upstairs."

No! I thought. *Please* don't let it be true!

I was afraid to look up. I knew what I'd see.

The door wide open. Mona, Ceecee, Rosie and Tara, staring at me in my underwear!

I forced myself to look. It was worse than I'd thought.

There they all stood—staring and laughing!

Tara laughed hardest of all. She laughed like a rotten little hyena.

You think that's bad? Wait. There's more.

Two days before the underwear disaster, I was

hanging around after school, playing basketball in the gym with Josh, Henry, and some other guys, including Kevin Flowers.

Kevin is a good player, big and tough. He is twice as tall as me! He loves basketball. The Duke Blue Devils are his favourite college team. He wears a Blue Devils cap to school every day.

While we were shooting baskets, I spied Tara hanging around the sidelines, where we'd all tossed our jackets and backpacks against the wall.

I got a bad feeling. I always do when Tara's around.

What's she doing there? I wondered.

Maybe her teacher kept her after school, and she's waiting for me to walk her home.

She's just trying to distract me, I told myself. Don't let her. Don't think about her. Just concentrate on the game.

I felt good. I actually sank a few baskets before the game ended. My side won. We had Kevin Flowers on our team, that's why.

We all jogged to the wall to get our packs. Tara was gone.

Funny, I thought. I guess she went home without me.

I hoisted my pack over my shoulder and said, "See you tomorrow, guys."

But Kevin's voice boomed through the gym. "Nobody move!"

We all froze.

"Where's my cap?" he demanded. "My Blue Devils cap is missing!"

I shrugged. *I* didn't know where his stupid cap was.

"Somebody took my cap," Kevin insisted. "Nobody leaves until we find it."

He grabbed Henry's backpack and started pawing through it. Everyone knows how much Henry loves that cap.

But Josh pointed at me. "Hey—what's that hanging out of Webster's pack?" he asked.

"My pack?" I cried. I glanced over my shoulder.

I saw a patch of blue sticking out of the zippered pocket.

My stomach lurched.

Kevin strode over to me and ripped the cap out of my pack.

"I don't know how it got there, Kevin," I insisted. "I swear—"

Kevin didn't wait to hear my excuses. He never was much of a listener.

I'll spare you the blood and gore. Let's just say my clothes didn't fit too well when Kevin got through taking me apart!

Josh and Henry helped me home. My mum didn't recognize me. My eyes and nose had traded places with my chin.

While I was in the bathroom cleaning myself

up, I caught a glimpse of Tara in the mirror. The bratty grin on her face told me all I needed to know.

"*You!*" I cried. "You put Kevin's cap in my pack! Didn't you!"

Tara just grinned. Yeah. She did it, all right.

"Why?" I demanded. "Why did you do it, Tara?"

Tara shrugged and tried to look innocent. "Was that Kevin's cap?" she said. "I thought it was yours."

"What a lie!" I cried. "I never wear a Duke cap, and you know it! You did that on purpose!"

I was so furious, I couldn't stand to look at her. I slammed the bathroom door in her face.

And of course I got in trouble for slamming the door.

Now you understand what I had to live with.

Now you know why I did the terrible thing that I did.

Anyone in my place would have done the same.

I stayed in my room that night, thinking hard. Plotting a way to get Tara in trouble.

But nothing came to me. At least, nothing good enough.

Then the clock arrived. A few days later, Tara did something that gave me an idea.

Tara couldn't stay away from the cuckoo clock. One afternoon, Dad caught Tara playing with the clock hands. She didn't get into any *real* trouble, of course—not sweet little Tara. But Dad did say, "I've got my eye on you, young lady. No more playing with the clock."

At last! I thought. At last Dad realizes that Tara's not a perfect angel. And at last I've found a way to get her into big trouble.

If something went wrong with the clock, I knew Tara would be blamed for it.

So I decided to make sure something *did* go wrong.

Tara deserved to get into trouble for the

hundreds of terrible things she did to me.

So *what* if just once she gets blamed for something she didn't do? I thought. It's only evening the score a little.

That night, after everybody was asleep, I sneaked downstairs to the den.

It was almost midnight. I crept up to the clock and waited.

One minute to go.

Thirty seconds.

Ten seconds.

Six, five, four, three, two, one . . .

The gong sounded.

Cuckoo! Cuckoo!

The yellow bird popped out. I grabbed it mid-cuckoo. It made short, strangling noises.

I twisted its head around, so it faced backwards. It looked really funny that way.

It finished out its twelve cuckoos, facing the wrong way.

I laughed to myself. When Dad saw it, he'd go *ballistic*!

The cuckoo slid back into its little window, still facing backwards.

This is going to drive Dad insane! I thought wickedly.

He'll be furious at Tara. He'll explode like a volcano!

Finally, Tara will know what it feels like to be blamed for something you didn't do.

I crept back upstairs. Not a sound. No one saw me.

I fell asleep that night a happy guy. There's nothing like revenge.

I slept late the next morning. I couldn't wait to see Dad blow up at Tara. I just hoped I hadn't missed it already.

I hurried downstairs. I checked the den.

The door stood open.

No one there. No sign of trouble yet.

Good, I thought. I haven't missed it.

I made my way into the kitchen, hungry. Mum, Dad and Tara sat around the table, piled with empty breakfast dishes.

As soon as they saw me, their faces lit up.

"Happy birthday!" they cried all at once.

"Very funny," I snapped. I opened a cabinet. "Is there any more cereal left?"

"Cereal!" Mum said. "Don't you want something special, like pancakes?"

I scratched my head. "Well, sure. Pancakes would be great."

This was a little strange. Usually if I woke up late, Mum said I had to get my own breakfast. And why should I want something special, anyway?

Mum mixed a fresh batch of pancake batter. "Don't go in the garage, Michael! Whatever you

295

do, don't go in the garage!" She hopped up and down, all excited. Just as if it were my birthday again.

Weird.

"... there's a huge mound of rubbish in there," Mum was saying. "It really stinks. It smells so bad, you could get sick from it!"

"Mum, what's with the rubbish story?" I asked. "I didn't believe it the first time."

"Just don't go into the garage," she repeated.

Why was she saying this to me? Why was she acting so weird?

Dad excused himself, saying, "I've got a few important chores to do," in a strange, jolly way.

I shrugged and tried to eat my breakfast in peace. But after breakfast I passed through the dining room. Somebody had decorated it with crêpe paper. One strand had been torn down.

Weird. Totally weird.

Dad came into the room, toolbox in hand. He picked up the torn piece of crêpe paper and started to tape it back up again.

"Why won't this crêpe paper stay up?" he asked.

"Dad," I said. "Why are you covering the dining room with crêpe paper?"

Dad smiled. "Because it's your birthday, of course! Every birthday party needs crêpe paper.

Now, I bet you can't wait to see your present, right?"

I stared at him.

What's going on here? I wondered.

Mum and Dad led me to the garage. Tara
followed. They all acted as if they were really
going to give me a birthday present.

Dad opened the garage door.

There it was. The bike.

It was perfectly shiny and new-looking. No
scratches anywhere.

That must be a surprise, I thought. They
figured out a way to get rid of the scratch
somehow. Or maybe they got me another new
bike!

"Do you like it?" Mum asked.

"It's awesome!" I replied.

Tara said, "Cool bike, Mike. Mum, I want one
of these for *my* birthday."

Then she jumped up on the seat. The bike fell
over on her. When we pulled it up, it had a big
scratch on it.

Mum cried, "Tara! Are you hurt?"

I couldn't believe it. What a nightmare!

It was happening all over again. Exactly as it had happened on my birthday.

What's going on?

"What's wrong, Michael?" Dad asked. "Don't you like the bike?"

What could I say? I felt sick. I felt so confused.

Then it dawned on me.

It must have been my wish, I thought.

My birthday wish.

After Tara tripped me and I fell on my cake, I wished I could go back in time and start my birthday all over again.

Somehow my wish came true.

Wow! I thought. This is kind of cool.

"Let's go inside," Mum said. "The party guests will be here soon."

The party?

Oh, no.

Please no!

Do I have to live through that horrible party again?

Yes.

Yes, I had to live through the whole horrible nightmare again.

My friends all showed up, just like the first time.

I heard Tara say the awful words, "Hey, Mona. You know, Michael really likes you."

Mona said, "He does?"

You already knew that, Mona, I thought. Tara told you four days ago.

You were standing in that very same spot. Wearing those same pink dungarees.

Mona, Ceecee and Rosie cracked up.

I panicked. This can't go on, I thought.

My mother came in, carrying a tray of soda. I grabbed her.

"Mum," I begged. "Please take Tara away. Shut her up in her room or something!"

"Michael, why? Your sister wants to have fun, too."

"Mum—*please!*"

"Oh, Michael, you're being silly. Be nice to Tara. She won't bother you. She's just a little girl."

Mum left the room, stranding me with Tara and my friends.

She couldn't save me.

No one could.

I showed the guys my new bike. Henry said, "Hey, what's this big scratch?"

When we got back to the living room, there were all my presents, opened by Tara.

"Look what Mona gave you, Michael!" Tara shouted.

I know, I know, I thought. A CD. With great love songs on it.

"I've heard there are some great *love* songs on it," Tara repeated.

Everybody laughed.

It was just as bad as before.

No. Worse. Because I could see it all coming. And I couldn't stop it.

Could I?

"Michael," Mum called. "Come into the kitchen, please. It's time for the birthday cake!"

Here's the test, I thought, dragging myself into the kitchen.

I'll carry in the cake—but this time I won't trip.

I know Tara is going to try and trip me. I won't
let her.

I won't make a fool of myself this time.

I don't have to. I don't have to repeat everything the same way.

Do I?

I stood in the kitchen, staring at the cake. I could hear my friends laughing and talking in the dining room. Tara was in there, too.

I knew she was standing just beyond the dining room door, waiting. Waiting to stick out her foot and trip me. Waiting to make me fall on my face and embarrass myself all over again.

Not this time.

I carefully picked up the cake in both hands. I started towards the dining room.

Mum followed, just as before.

I stopped in front of the entrance to the dining room. I glanced down.

No sign of Tara's foot.

Carefully, watching closely, I stepped through the door. One step.

So far, so good.

Another step. I stood inside the dining room now.

I'd made it! All I had to do was get to the table, about five steps away, and I'd be safe.

I took another step forward. Another.

Then I felt a tug on my foot.

Tara reached out from under the table.

So that was where she'd been hiding. I knew it now. But it was too late.

Everything seemed to move in slow motion. Like in a dream.

I heard an evil giggle.

She grabbed my foot.

Oh, no, I thought. It's happened.

I lost my balance.

As I fell, I turned my head and glanced back.

Tara sat under that table, smirking at me.

I wanted to kill her.

But first I had to fall on my face on a cake.

The cake flew out of my arms. I turned my head again.

Splat!

Everybody gasped with laughter. I sat up and wiped the frosting from my eyes.

Mona leaned over the table, laughing harder than anybody.

The second time was more embarrassing than the first.

I sat on the floor, my face covered with cake, thinking, how could I have been so stupid?

Why did I have to make that wish?

I'll never wish for anything ever again.

I cleaned myself up and managed to survive the rest of the party. When I went to bed that night, I thought, at least it's over.

I switched off the light and pulled the covers up high.

It's over, I repeated. I'll go to sleep, and everything will be back to normal in the morning.

I shut my eyes and fell asleep. But in my dreams, all night long, I saw scenes from my horrible birthday party. The nightmare party became a real nightmare.

There was Tara, telling Mona that I liked her. Mona's face loomed up large in my dreams, laughing, laughing. Ceecee and Rosie and the guys, all laughing right in my face.

I tripped and fell on top of the cake, over and over again.

I tossed and turned. Each dream was scarier than the last. Soon my friends looked like horrible monsters. And Tara was the most horrible of all. Her features melted into a blur as she laughed and laughed at me.

Wake up, I told myself. Wake up!

I dragged myself out of the nightmare world. I sat up in bed, in a cold sweat.

The room was still dark. I glanced at the clock.

305

Three o'clock in the morning.

I can't sleep, I thought miserably. I can't calm down.

I've got to tell Mum and Dad what happened. Maybe they can help.

Maybe they can make me feel better.

I climbed out of bed and hurried down the dark hall to their room. Their door was open a crack.

I pushed it open.

"Mum? Dad? Are you awake?"

Dad rolled over and grunted, "Huh?"

I shook Mum's shoulder. "Mum?"

Mum stirred. "What is it, Michael?" she whispered. She sat up and grabbed the clock radio. In the clock's dim blue glow I saw her squint, trying to read the time.

"It's three o'clock!" she cried.

Dad snorted and sat up suddenly. "Huh? What?"

"Mum, you've got to listen to me!" I whispered. "Something creepy happened today. Didn't you notice it?"

"Michael, what is this—"

"My birthday," I explained. "Tara ruined my birthday, and I wished I could have it all over again. I wanted to make it better. But I never thought the wish would come true! Then, today, it was my birthday again! And everything happened exactly the same. It was horrible!"

Dad rubbed his eyes. "That you, Michael?"

Mum patted him. "Go back to sleep, dear, Michael's just had a bad dream."

"No, Mum," I cried. "It wasn't a dream. It was real! My birthday happened twice! You were there, both times. Don't you understand?"

"Listen, Michael," Mum began. I heard impatience in her voice. "I know you're excited about your birthday, but it's two days away. Only two days to go—then it will be your birthday at last! Okay? So go back to bed now and get some sleep."

She kissed me good night. "Only two days till your birthday. Sweet dreams."

I staggered back to bed, my head spinning.

Two days until my birthday?

Hadn't I just lived through my birthday—twice?

I switched on the reading lamp and stared at the date on my watch. February third, it said.

My birthday is February fifth. My birthday was two days away.

Could it be true? Was time going backwards?

No, I thought. I must be going nuts.

I shook my head hard. I slapped myself a few times. Going back in time. I laughed at the idea.

It's impossible, I thought. Get a hold of yourself, Michael.

All I did was wish to celebrate my birthday over again—*once*.

I didn't wish to repeat my twelfth birthday

308

for the rest of my life!

But if that's what's happening, why is it now *two* days before my birthday? Why isn't it just the night before?

Maybe time really *is* going backwards, I thought. Maybe this has nothing to do with my wish.

But, then—why is this happening to me?

I racked my brains.

The clock. Dad's cuckoo clock.

I twisted the cuckoo's head backwards...went to bed . . . and when I woke up, time had gone backwards.

Could that be it? Did *I* do this?

Is Dad's clock really magic?

Maybe I shouldn't have turned that stupid bird backwards, I decided. It figures—I try to get Tara in trouble, and end up getting *myself* into a horrible mess.

Well, if that *is* what happened, it's easy enough to fix.

I'll just go downstairs and turn the cuckoo's head back around.

I tiptoed out of my room and down the stairs. My parents had probably fallen back to sleep already, but I didn't want to take any chances.

I definitely didn't want Dad to catch me fooling around with his precious clock.

My feet hit the cold, bare floor of the hall.

**I crept into the den. I switched on a lamp.
I glanced around the room.
The cuckoo clock was gone!**

310

"No!" I cried.

Had the clock been stolen?

Without the clock, how could I fix everything? How could I turn the bird's head around and make my life go forward again?

I raced upstairs. I didn't care who I woke up now.

"Mum! Dad!" I yelled. I burst into their room and shook Mum awake again.

"Michael, what is it?" She sounded furious. "It's the middle of the night. We're trying to get some sleep!"

Let them be angry, I thought. This was way more important.

"The cuckoo clock! It's gone!"

Dad rolled over. "What? Huh?"

"Michael, you've had another nightmare," Mum assured me.

"It's not a nightmare, Mum—it's true! Go downstairs and see for yourself! There's no

311

cuckoo clock in the den!"

"Michael—listen to me. It was a dream."
Mum's voice was firm. "We don't own a cuckoo
clock. We never did."

I staggered backwards.

"It's just a dream. A bad dream," she said.

"But Dad bought it . . ."

I stopped.

I understood now.

The date was February third. Two days before
my birthday.

And *five* days before Dad bought the cuckoo
clock.

We were travelling back in time. Dad hadn't
bought the clock yet.

I felt sick.

Mum said, "Michael, are you all right?" She
climbed out of bed and pressed the back of her
hand against my forehead.

"You feel a little warm," she said, nicer
now that she thought I might be sick. "Come
on, let's get you to bed. I'll bet you have a fever—
and that's why you're having all these night-
mares."

Dad grunted again. "What? Sick?"

"I'll take care of it, Herman," Mum whispered.
"Go back to sleep."

She guided me back to bed. She thought I was
sick.

But I knew the truth.

I had made time move backwards. And the clock was gone.

How would I fix things now?

By the time I got to the kitchen the next morning, Mum, Dad and Tara had already eaten.

"Hurry up, Michael," Dad said. "You'll be late."

Being late for school didn't seem to matter much at the moment.

"Dad, please sit down for a second," I pleaded. "Just for a minute. It's important."

Dad sat, impatiently, on the edge of a kitchen chair. "Michael, what is it?"

"Mum, are you listening?" I asked.

"Sure, honey," Mum said. She put the milk in the refrigerator and busily wiped off the counter.

"This is going to sound weird," I began. "But I'm not kidding."

I paused. Dad waited. I could tell by the tension in his face he expected me to say something totally dopey.

I didn't disappoint him.

"Dad, time is going backwards. Every day I wake up—and it's an earlier day than the last!"

Dad's face drooped. "Michael, you have a wonderful imagination, but I'm really running late. Can we talk about it when I get home from work tonight? Or why don't you write it down? You know I love reading science fiction stories."

"But, Dad—"

Mum said, "Did somebody remember to feed the cat?"

"*I* did it," Tara said. "Even though it's *supposed* to be *Michael's* job."

"Thanks, Tara," Mum said. "Let's hit the road, everybody."

I grabbed a muffin as Mum hustled us out the door.

They're too busy to understand right now, I reasoned as I hurried to school. Tonight, at dinner, when I have more time to explain . . .

I had lots of time to think about my problem during school. I'd lived through this day before, too. I'd already done all the work, heard all the lessons, eaten the lousy lunch.

When my maths teacher, Mr Parker, turned his back to the class, I knew what would happen next. I predicted it to the second. Kevin Flowers threw an eraser at him and hit him smack on the back of his black trousers.

Now Mr Parker is going to turn around . . . I thought, watching Mr Parker.

He turned around.

. . . now he'll yell at Kevin . . .

Mr Parker shouted, "Kevin Flowers—to the principal's office, now!"

. . . now Kevin will start yelling his head off.

"How do you know it was me!" Kevin yelled. "You didn't see me do anything!"

The rest of the scene happened as I remembered it. Mr Parker cowered a bit—Kevin is pretty big—but told Kevin to go to the principal's office again. Kevin kicked over an empty chair and threw his books across the room.

It was all so boring.

After school, I found Tara in the den, teasing Bubba. She lifted his hind legs and made him walk on his front paws.

"Tara, stop it!" I cried. I tried to take Bubba away from her. She let the cat go. Bubba meowed and scratched me across the arm.

"Ow!" I dropped Bubba. He ran away.

It felt very familiar. And painful.

"Michael, what were you doing to that cat?" Mum demanded.

"Nothing! He scratched me!"

"Stop teasing him, and he won't scratch you," Mum scolded.

The doorbell rang.

Oh, no.

Mona, Ceecee and Rosie. *The Frog Prince.*

The underwear.

315

I can't let it happen.

But my feet started taking me upstairs. I was walking like a robot to my room.

Why am I doing this? I asked myself.

I'll get my frog costume. The zipper will be stuck.

Tara will open the door, and I'll be standing there in my underpants.

Mona will laugh her head off. I'll want to sink through the floor.

I know all this will happen.

So why am I doing it?

Can't I stop myself?

Don't go upstairs, I begged myself. Don't go to your room.

You don't *have* to do this.

There must be a way to stop it, to control it.

I forced myself to turn around. I walked back down the steps. I sat down on the third step.

Tara answered the door, and soon the girls stood before me in the hall.

Okay, I thought. I'm controlling it. Already things are happening differently from before.

"Michael, where's your costume?" Mona asked. "I really want to see what your costume looks like."

"Uh, no you don't," I said, shrinking a little. "It's really ugly, and I don't want to scare you girls—"

"Don't be a jerk, Michael," Ceecee said. "Why would we be scared by a stupid frog costume?"

"And, anyway, I want to rehearse with it," Mona added. "I don't want to see the costume for the first time on-stage. I'll need to be prepared for it. I need to practise with the costume—and you in it."

"Come on, Michael," Tara put in. "Show them the costume. I want to see it, too."

I flashed her a dirty look. I knew what she had in mind.

"No," I insisted. "I can't do that."

"Why not?" Mona demanded.

"I just can't."

"He's shy!" Rosie exclaimed.

"He's embarrassed," Tara added.

"No, it's not that," I said. "It's just that . . . it's awfully hot in that costume, and—"

Mona leaned close to me. I smelled something sweet, like strawberries. It must've been the shampoo she used. "Come on, Michael," she said. "For me?"

"No."

She stamped her foot. "I won't rehearse our scenes unless you put on that costume!"

I sighed. I didn't see any way out of it.

Mona wouldn't leave me alone until I put on that frog costume.

I gave in. "Okay."

"Hurray!" Tara cried. I gave her another dirty look.

All right, I thought. I may have put on the

costume. But that doesn't mean the girls have to see me in my underwear.

I can still keep that from happening.

I trudged up to my room. But this time, I locked the door.

Now try to embarrass me, Tara, I thought. You can't outsmart Michael Webster. No way.

The door was locked. I felt sure I was safe.

I took off my jeans and my shirt. I dragged the frog costume out of the closet.

I tugged on the zipper. It was stuck.

Just like the last time.

But this time it's okay, I told myself. The door is locked. I have privacy.

Then the door flew open.

I stood helplessly in my underwear. Mona, Rosie and Ceecee stared at me. Then they screamed and started laughing.

"Tara!" I yelled. "The door was locked!"

"No, it wasn't," Tara replied. "The lock's broken, remember?"

"No!" I cried. "Dad fixed it . . . he fixed it . . ."

I tried to remember when Dad had fixed the lock on my bedroom door.

Oh, right.

It was after the underwear nightmare. On my birthday.

So it hadn't happened yet.

How was I supposed to keep all this straight?

Oh, no, I thought. I'm doomed.

Time is all messed up. And I have no way of stopping it.

I began to shake. This was too frightening.

Where would it end? I had no idea. It was getting scarier by the minute.

I could hardly eat dinner that night. I'd eaten it before, of course, and hadn't liked it the first time. Peas, carrots and mushrooms. With brown rice.

I picked at the rice and the carrots. I never eat peas. I slipped them into my napkin when Mum and Dad weren't looking.

I watched Mum, Dad and Tara eat dinner as if nothing were wrong. They sat calmly around the table, saying the same things they'd said last time.

Mum and Dad must notice that something is weird, I thought. They must.

So why don't they say anything about it?

I waited for Dad to finish telling us about his day at work. Then I brought up the subject again. I decided to take it slowly.

"Mum? Dad? Doesn't this dinner seem a little bit familiar?"

"I'll say," Dad replied. "It reminds me of the lunch we ate at that vegetarian restaurant last month. Ugh."

Mum glared at him, then at me. "What are you trying to tell us, Michael?" she said frostily. "Are you tired of eating healthy food?"

"I am," Dad said.

"Me, too," Tara chimed in.

"No. No way," I insisted. "You don't understand. I don't mean that we've eaten food like this before. I mean that we have eaten *this very meal* before. We're eating it twice."

Dad frowned. "No weird theories at the dinner table, please, Michael."

They weren't getting it. I ploughed ahead. "It's not just this dinner. It's this whole day. Haven't you noticed? We're doing everything over! Time is going backwards!"

"Shut up, Michael," Tara said. "This is so boring. Can't we talk about something else?"

"Tara," Mum scolded, "don't say 'shut up'." She turned to me. "Have you been reading those comic books again?"

I grew very frustrated. "You're not listening to me!" I cried. "Tomorrow is going to be yesterday, and the day after that will be the day before! Everything is going backwards!"

Mum and Dad exchanged glances. They seemed to be sharing a secret.

They *do* know something, I thought with excitement. They know something, but they're afraid to tell me.

Mum gazed at me very seriously. "All right, Michael. We might as well tell you," she said. "We're all caught in a time warp, and there's nothing we can do about it."

Mum pushed back her chair. She walked backwards to the stove. She started dishing rice from her plate into the pot on the stove.

"Yenoh, ecir erom?" she asked Dad.

Huh?

"Esaelp, sey," Dad replied.

"Oot, em," Tara said. She spat some rice out on her fork and dumped it back on her plate. She was eating backwards!

Dad stood up and walked backwards to Mum. Then Tara skipped backwards around the kitchen table.

They were all talking and moving backwards. We really *were* in a time warp!

"Hey!" I cried. "It's true!"

Why wasn't I talking backwards, too?

"Norom," Tara said.

She cracked up first. Then Dad started laughing. Then Mum.

I finally caught on. It was a joke. "You—

323

you're all *horrible*!" I cried.

That made them laugh even more.

"I was wondering when you'd figure it out," Tara sneered.

They all sat down at the table again. Mum couldn't help grinning. "We're sorry, Michael. We didn't mean to make fun of you."

"Yes we did!" Tara exclaimed.

I stared at them in horror.

This was the most terrible thing that had ever happened to me. And my parents thought it was a big joke.

Then Dad said, "Michael, did you ever hear of *déjà vu*?"

I shook my head.

"It's when something happens to you and you have the feeling it's happened before," he explained. "Everyone feels that way once in a while. It's nothing to be afraid of."

"Maybe you're nervous about something," Mum added. "Like your birthday coming up. I'll bet you're a little nervous about turning twelve, right? And planning your party and everything?"

"Not really," I protested. "I know that feeling. But this isn't the same thing! This is—"

"Say, Mike," Dad interrupted. "Wait till you see what I got you for your birthday. You're going to flip! It's a big surprise."

No, it isn't, I thought unhappily.

324

It's not a surprise at all. You've given me that birthday present twice already. How many times are you going to give me that stupid bike?

"Mum, Michael is hiding peas in his napkin again," Tara ratted.

I smushed the peas up in my napkin and threw it in her face.

When I went to school the next morning, I wasn't sure what day it was. It was getting hard to keep track. My classes, my lunch, the stuff my friends said all seemed familiar. But nothing unusual happened. It could have been any day of the school year.

I played basketball after school that day, as usual. While I was playing, a funny feeling crept over me.

A bad feeling.

I've already played this game, I realized. And it didn't end well.

But I kept on playing, waiting to see what would happen.

My team won. We collected our packs.

Then Kevin Flowers yelled, "Where's my Blue Devils cap?"

Oh, yeah, I remembered.

This was *that* basketball game. How could I forget?

Good old Tara. She's done it again!

"Nobody leaves until we find that cap!"

I shut my eyes and handed over my pack.

I knew what was coming. Might as well get it over with.

Getting pounded to a pulp by Kevin Flowers hurt a lot. But at least the pain didn't last long.

The next morning when I woke up, it was all gone. The pain, the scabs, the bruises, everything.

What day is it today? I wondered. It must be a few days before Kevin beat me up.

I hope I won't have to live through that a third time.

But what will happen today?

As I walked to school, I searched for clues. I tried to remember what had happened a day or two before Kevin beat me up.

A maths test? Maybe. I hoped not. But at least it would be easier this time around. I could even try to remember what the problems were and look up all the answers before the test!

I was a little late today. Did that mean something? I wondered. Would I get into trouble?

My form teacher, Ms Jacobson, had closed the classroom door. I opened it. The classroom was already full.

Ms Jacobson didn't look up when I walked in.

I must not be that late, I thought. Guess I won't get in trouble after all.

I started for the back of the room, where I usually sit. As I passed through the rows of desks, I glanced at the other kids.

Who's that guy? I wondered, staring at a chubby, blond kid I'd never seen before.

Then I noticed a pretty girl with cornrows and three earrings in one ear. I'd never seen her before, either.

I stared at all the faces in the classroom. None of the kids looked familiar.

What's going on? I wondered, feeling panic choke my throat.

I don't know *any* of these kids!

Where's my class?

Ms Jacobson finally turned around. She stared at me.

"Hey," the blond kid shouted. "What's a third-grader doing in here?"

Everybody laughed. I couldn't understand why.

A third-grader? Who was he talking about?

I didn't see any third-graders.

"You're in the wrong classroom, young man," Ms Jacobson said to me. She opened the door, showing me the way out.

"I think your room is downstairs on the second floor," she added.

"Thanks," I said. I didn't know what she was talking about. But I decided to go along with her.

She shut the door behind her. I could hear the kids laughing behind the door. I hurried down the hall to the boy's bathroom. I needed to splash some cold water on my face. Maybe that would help.

I turned on the cold water tap. Then I glanced in the mirror, very quickly.

The mirror seems a little higher than usual, I thought.

I washed my hands in the cold water and splashed some on my face.

The sink seems higher, too, I noticed. Strange.

Am I in the right school?

I glanced in the mirror again—and got the shock of my life.

Was that *me*?

I looked so *young*.

I ran my hand through my short, brushlike brown hair. That dopey crew cut I'd had all through the third grade.

I don't believe it, I thought, shaking my head. I'm a third-grader again!

I've got my third-grade hair. My third-grade clothes. My third-grade body.

But my seventh-grade brain. I think.

Third grade.

That means I've slipped back four years—in one night.

My whole body started to tremble. I grabbed on to the sink to steady myself.

I was suddenly paralysed with fear.

Things were speeding up. Now I'd lost whole years in one night! How old will I be when I wake up tomorrow? I asked myself.

Time was going backward faster and faster—

and I still hadn't found a way to stop it!

I shut off the water and dried my face with a paper towel. I didn't know what to do. I was so frightened, I couldn't think straight.

I walked back to my third-grade classroom.

First I glanced through the window of the classroom door. There she was, Mrs Harris, my old third-grade teacher. I'd know that helmet of silver hair anywhere.

And I knew, as soon as I saw her, that I really *had* gone back in time four years.

Because old Mrs Harris shouldn't have been in school that day. She'd retired two years earlier. When I was in fifth grade.

I opened the door and stepped into the classroom.

Mrs Harris didn't bat an eye. "Take a seat, Michael," she commanded. She never mentioned the fact that I was late.

Mrs Harris always liked me.

I checked out the other kids in the class. I saw Henry, Josh, Ceecee and Mona, all little third-graders now.

Mona wore her shiny brown hair in two braids. Ceecee wore hers in one of those stupid side ponytails.

Josh didn't have pimples on his forehead, I noticed. Henry had a sticker on the back of his hand—Donatello, from the Teenage Mutant Hero Turtles.

It was my class all right.

I sat down at an empty desk in the back. My old desk. Right next to Henry.

I glanced at him. He was picking his nose.

Gross. I'd forgotten about that part of being a third-grader.

"Michael, we're on page thirty-three in your spelling book," Mrs Harris informed me.

I reached inside the desk and found my spelling book. I opened it to page thirty-three.

"These are the words you'll need to know for tomorrow's spelling test," Mrs Harris announced. She wrote the words on the board, even though we could read them right there in the spelling book: *Taste, sense, grandmother, easy, happiness*.

"Man," Henry whispered to me. "These words are tough. Look how many letters there are in *grandmother*!"

I didn't know what to say to him. On my last spelling test (when I was still in the seventh grade), I'd had to spell *psychology*. *Grandmother* wasn't a big challenge for me any more.

I zoned out for most of the day. I'd always wished school were easier, but not *this* easy. It was so babyish and boring.

Lunch and break were even worse. Josh chewed up a banana and stuck his tongue out at me. Henry painted his face with chocolate pudding.

331

Finally the school day ended. I dragged my little third-grade body home.

When I opened the front door, I heard a horrible screech. Bubba, just a kitten now, raced past me and out the door. Tara toddled after him.

"Don't tease the cat," I scolded her.

"You're dumb," she replied.

I stared at Tara. She was three years old.

I tried to remember. Had I liked her better when she was three?

"Give me a piggyback!" she cried, tugging on my backpack.

"Get off me," I said.

My pack dropped to the floor. I stooped to pick it up. She grabbed a hunk of my hair and yanked it.

"Ow!" I screamed.

She laughed and laughed.

"That hurt!" I yelled, and shoved her—just as Mum stepped into the hall.

She rushed to Tara's side. "Michael, don't shove your sister. She's only a little girl!"

I stormed off to my room to think.

No, I *hadn't* liked Tara better when she was three. She was as much of a brat as ever.

She was born a brat, and she'd never grow out of it, I knew. She'd be a brat for the rest of her life, driving me crazy even when we're old.

If we ever get to be old, I thought with a

shudder. We'll *never* grow up at this rate.

What am I going to do? I worried. I've slipped back in time four years! If I don't do something fast, I'll be a baby again.

And then what?

A cold shiver ran down my back.

And then what? I asked myself.

Will I disappear *completely*?

I woke up in a panic every morning.

What day was it? What *year* was it?

I had no idea.

I climbed out of bed—it seemed farther away from the floor than it used to—and padded across the hall to the bathroom.

I stared in the mirror. How old was I? Younger than I'd been the day before, I knew that much.

I went back to my room and began to get dressed. Mum had left my clothes for the day folded on a chair in my room.

I examined the jeans I was supposed to wear. They had a picture of a cowboy on the back pocket.

Oh, yeah, I remembered. *These* jeans. The cowboy jeans.

Second grade.

That means I must be seven years old now.

I stepped into the trousers, thinking, I can't believe I have to wear these stupid jeans again.

Then I unfolded the shirt Mum had picked out for me.

My heart sank when I saw it: A cowboy shirt—with fringe and everything.

This is so embarrassing, I thought. How could I have ever let Mum do this to me?

Deep down I knew that I used to like these clothes. I probably picked them out myself.

But I couldn't stand to admit that I'd ever been so stupid.

Downstairs, Tara was still in her pyjamas, watching cartoons. She was now two.

When she saw me pass through the living room, she held out her arms to me. "Kiss! Kiss!" she called.

She wanted me to kiss her? That didn't seem like Tara.

But maybe the two-year-old Tara was still sweet and innocent. Maybe, at two, Tara was actually likeable.

"Kiss! Kiss!" she begged.

"Give poor Tara a kiss," Mum called from the kitchen. "You're her big brother, Michael. She looks up to you."

I sighed. "Okay."

I leaned down to give Tara a kiss on the cheek. With one chubby index finger, she poked me in the eye.

"Ow!" I shrieked.

Tara laughed.

Same old terrible Tara, I thought as I stumbled into the kitchen, one hand over my sore eye.

She was born bad!

This time, at school, I knew which classroom to go to.

There sat all my old friends, Mona and everybody, younger than ever. I'd forgotten how dopey everybody used to look when we were little.

I sat through another dull day of learning stuff I already knew. Subtraction. How to read books with really big print. Perfecting my capital L.

At least it gave me lots of time to think.

Every day I tried to figure out what to do. But I never came up with an answer.

Then I remembered Dad telling us he'd been wanting the cuckoo clock for fifteen years.

Fifteen years! That's it! The clock must be at that antique shop!

I'll go and find the clock, I decided. I couldn't wait for school to end that day.

I figured if I could turn the cuckoo around, time would go forward again. I knew the dial that showed the year must be going backwards, too. All I had to do was reset the date on the clock to the right year, and I'd be twelve again.

I missed being twelve. Seven-year-olds don't

get away with much. Someone's always watching you.

When the school day ended, I started down the block towards my house. I knew the crossing guard was watching me, making sure I'd get home safely.

But at the second block I dashed around the corner to the bus stop. I hoped the crossing guard hadn't seen me.

I stood behind a tree, trying not to be seen.

A few minutes later, a bus pulled over. The doors opened with a hiss. I stepped aboard.

The bus driver eyed me strangely. "Aren't you a little young to be catching the bus by yourself?" he asked me.

"Mind your own business," I replied.

He looked startled, so I added, "I'm meeting Daddy at his office. Mummy said it was okay."

He nodded and let the doors slide shut.

I started to put three quarters in the coin slot, but the driver stopped me after two.

"Whoa, there, buddy," he said, pressing the third quarter into my palm. "Fare's only fifty cents. Keep this quarter for a phone call."

"Oh, yeah. Right." I'd forgotten. They raised the bus fare to 75 cents when I was eleven. But now I was only seven. I put the quarter in my pocket.

The bus pulled away from the kerb and chugged downtown.

I remembered hearing Dad say that Anthony's Antiques and Stuff was across the street from his office. I got off the bus at Dad's block.

I hoped Dad wouldn't see me. I knew I'd be in big trouble if he did.

I wasn't allowed to catch the bus by myself when I was seven.

I hurried past Dad's building and crossed the street. On the corner stood a construction site; just a pile of bricks and rubble, really. Further down the block I saw a black sign with ANTHONY'S ANTIQUES AND STUFF painted on it in gold letters.

My heart began to pound.

I'm almost there, I thought. Soon everything will be all right.

I'll just walk into the shop and find the clock. Then, when no one's looking, I'll turn the cuckoo around and fix the year.

I won't have to worry about waking up tomorrow morning as a three-year-old or something. My life will go back to normal.

Life will seem so easy, I told myself, when time is moving forward the way it's supposed to. Even *with* Tara around!

I gazed through the big plate glass window of the shop. There it stood, right in the window. The clock.

My palms began to sweat, I felt so excited.

I hurried to the shop door and turned the handle.

It wouldn't move. I jiggled it harder.

The door was locked.

Then I noticed a sign, tucked in the bottom corner of the door.

It said, CLOSED FOR VACATION.

I let out a howl of frustration. "NOOO!" I cried. Tears sprang to my eyes. "No! Not after all this."

I banged my head against the door. I couldn't stand it.

Closed for vacation.

How could I have such terrible luck?

How long was Anthony planning to be on vacation? I wondered. How long will the shop be closed?

By the time it reopens, I could be a baby!

I gritted my teeth and thought, there's no way I'm letting that happen. No way!

I've got to do something. *Anything*.

I pressed my nose against the shop window. The cuckoo clock was standing there, a metre or so in front of me.

And I couldn't get to it.

The window stood between me and that clock. The window . . .

Normally, I would never think of doing what I decided to do at that moment.

But I was desperate. I had to reach that clock.

It really was a matter of life and death!

I strolled down the block to the construction site, trying to look casual. Trying not to look like a kid who was planning to break a shop window.

I stuffed my hands in the pockets of my cowboy jeans and whistled. I was sort of grateful to be wearing this stupid cowboy outfit after all. It made me look innocent.

Who would suspect a seven-year-old in a cowboy suit of trying to break into an antique shop?

I kicked around a little dirt at the construction site. Kicked a few rocks. Nobody seemed to be working there.

Slowly I made my way over to a pile of bricks. I glanced around to see if anybody saw me.

The coast was clear.

I picked up a brick and hefted it in my hand. It was very heavy. It wouldn't be easy for me, in my little second-grade body, to throw it far.

But I didn't have to throw it far. Just through the window.

I tried stuffing the brick in my jeans pocket, but it was too big. So I carried it in both hands back to the shop.

I tried to look as if it were perfectly normal for a boy to be carrying a brick down the street.

A few adults quickly passed by. No one gave me a second glance.

I stood in front of the shiny plate glass window, weighing the brick in my hand. I wondered if a burglar alarm would go off when I broke the window.

Would I be arrested?

Maybe it wouldn't matter. If I made time to go to the present, I'd escape the police.

Be brave, I told myself. Go for it!

With both hands, I raised the brick over my head . . .

. . . and someone grabbed me from behind.

"Help!" I shouted. I spun around. "Dad!"

"Michael, what are you doing here?" Dad demanded. "Are you by yourself?"

I let the brick fall to the pavement. He didn't seem to see it.

"I—I wanted to surprise you," I lied. "I wanted to come and visit you after school."

He stared at me as if he didn't quite understand. So I added, for good measure, "I missed you, Daddy."

He smiled. "You missed me?" He was touched. I could tell.

"How did you get here?" he asked. "On the bus?"

I nodded.

"You know you're not allowed to go on the bus by yourself," he said. But he didn't sound angry. I knew that line about missing him would soften him up.

Meanwhile, I still had the same major

343

problem—getting my hands on the cuckoo clock.

Could Dad help me? Would he? I was willing to try anything. "Dad," I said, "that clock—"

Dad put his arm around me. "Isn't it a beauty? I've been admiring it for years."

"Dad, I've got to get to the clock," I insisted. "It's very, very important! Do you know when the store will open again? We've got to get that clock somehow!"

Dad misunderstood me. He patted me on the head and said, "I know how you feel, Michael. I wish I could have the clock right now. But I can't afford it. Maybe some day . . ."

He pulled me away from the shop. "Come on— let's go home. I wonder what's for supper tonight?"

I didn't say another word all the way home in the car. All I could think about was the clock— and what would happen to me next.

How old will I be when I wake up tomorrow? I wondered.

Or how young?

17

When I opened my eyes the next morning, everything had changed.

The walls were painted baby blue. The bedspread and the curtains matched. The material was printed with bouncing kangaroos. On one wall hung a needlepoint picture of a cow.

It wasn't my room, but it looked familiar.

Then I felt a lump in the bed. I reached under the kangaroo covers and pulled out Harold, my old teddy bear.

I slowly understood. I was back in my old bedroom.

How had I ended up there? It was Tara's room now.

I jumped out of bed. I was wearing smurf pyjamas.

I swear I don't remember ever liking smurfs that much.

I ran to the bathroom to look in the mirror.

How old was I now?

I couldn't tell. I had to stand on the toilet seat to see my face.

A bad sign.

Yikes. I looked about five years old!

I hopped off the toilet seat and hurried downstairs.

"Hello, Mikey," Mum said, squeezing me and giving me a big kiss.

"Hi, Mummy," I said. I couldn't believe how babyish my voice sounded.

Dad sat at the kitchen table, drinking coffee. He put down his mug and held out his arms. "Come give Daddy a good morning kiss," he said.

I sighed and forced myself to run into his arms and kiss him on the cheek. I'd forgotten how many stupid things little kids have to put up with.

I ran out of the kitchen on my little five-year-old legs, through the living room, into the den, and back to the kitchen. Something was missing.

No, some*one* was missing.

Tara.

"Sit still for a minute, sweetie," Mum said, scooping me up and plopping me into a chair. "Want some cereal?"

"Where's Tara?" I demanded.

"Who?" Mum replied.

"Tara," I repeated.

346

Mum glanced at Dad. Dad shrugged.

"You know," I persisted. "My little sister."

Mum smiled. "Oh, *Tara*," she said, seeming to understand at last.

She glanced at Dad and mouthed, "Invisible friend."

"Huh?" Dad said out loud. "He has an invisible friend?"

Mum frowned at him and gave me a bowl of cereal. "What does your friend Tara look like, Mikey?"

I didn't answer her. I was too shocked to speak.

They don't know who I'm talking about! I realized.

Tara don't exist. She hasn't been born yet!

For a brief moment, I felt a thrill. No Tara! I could go through this whole day without ever seeing, hearing, or smelling Tara the Terrible! How totally awesome!

But then the real meaning of this sank in.

One Webster kid had disappeared.

I was next.

After I'd finished my cereal, Mum took me upstairs to get dressed. She put on my shirt and trousers and socks and shoes. She didn't tie the shoes, though.

"Okay, Mikey," she said. "Let's practise tying your shoes. Remember how we did it yesterday?"

She took my shoelaces in her fingers and, as she tied them, chanted. "The bunny hops *around* the tree and ducks *under* the bush. Remember?"

She sat back to watch me try to tie my other shoe. I could tell by the look on her face she didn't expect me to get very far.

I bent over and easily tied the shoe. I didn't have time to fool around with this stuff.

Mum stared at me in amazement.

"Come on, Mum, let's get going," I said, straightening up.

"Mikey!" Mum cried. "You did it! You tied your shoe for the first time!" She grabbed me and hugged me hard. "Wait till I tell Daddy!"

I followed her downstairs, rolling my eyes.

So I tied my shoe. Big deal!

"Honey!" Mum called. "Mikey tied his shoe— all by himself!"

"Hey!" Dad cried happily. He held up one hand so I could slap him five. "That's my big boy!"

This time I saw him mouth to Mum: "Took him long enough!"

I was too worried to be insulted.

Mum walked me to nursery school. She told my teacher that I'd learned to tie my shoe. Big excitement all around.

I had to sit around that stupid nursery all morning, finger-painting and singing the ABC song.

I knew I had to get back to that antique store. It was all I could think about.

I've *got* to change that cuckoo clock, I thought desperately. Who knows? Tomorrow I might not know how to walk.

But how would I get there? It had been hard enough to get into town as a second-grader. As a five-year-old, it would be nearly impossible.

And, besides, even if I could get on the bus without anybody asking questions, I didn't have any money with me.

I glanced at the teacher's purse. Maybe I could steal a couple of quarters from her. She'd probably never know.

But if she caught me, I'd be in really big trouble. And I had enough trouble now.

I decided to sneak on to the bus somehow. I knew I could find a way.

When the nursery torture was finally over for the day, I raced out of the building to catch the bus—

—and bumped smack into Mum.

"Hi, Mikey," she said. "Did you have a nice day?"

I forgot that she picked me up every day from nursery school.

She took my hand in her iron grip. There was no escape.

349

At least I'm here, I thought when I woke up the next morning. At least I'm still alive.

But I'm four years old.

Time is running out.

Mum waltzed into my room, singing, "Good morning to you, good morning to you, good morning dear Mikey, good morning to you! Ready for playgroup?"

Yuck. Playgroup.

Things kept getting worse and worse.

I couldn't take it any more. Mum dropped me off at playgroup with a kiss and her usual, "Have a nice day, Mikey!"

I stalked to the nearest corner and sat. I watched the other little kids play. I refused to do anything. No singing. No painting. No sandbox. No games for me.

"Michael, what's the matter with you today?" the teacher, Ms Sarton asked. "Don't you feel well?"

"I feel okay," I told her.

"Well, then, why aren't you playing?" She studied me for a minute, then added, "I think you need to play."

Without asking my permission or anything, she picked me up, carried me outside, and dumped me in the sandbox.

"Mona will play with you," she said brightly.

Mona was very cute when she was four. Why didn't I remember that?

Mona didn't say anything to me. She concentrated on the sand igloo she was building—at least I *think* it was supposed to be an igloo. It was round, anyway. I started to say hi to her, but suddenly felt shy.

Then I caught myself. Why should I feel bashful with a four-year-old girl?

Anyway, I reasoned, she hasn't seen me in my underwear yet. That won't happen for another eight years.

"Hi, Mona," I said. I cringed when I heard the babyish playgroup voice that came out of my mouth. But everyone else seemed to be used to it.

Mona turned up her nose. "Eeew," she sniffed. "A boy. I hate boys."

"Well," I squeaked in my little boy voice, "if that's the way you feel, forget I said anything."

351

Mona stared at me now, as if she didn't quite understand what I had said.

"You're stupid," she said.

I shrugged and began to draw swirls in the sand with my chubby little finger. Mona dug a moat around her sand igloo. Then she stood up. "Don't let anybody smash my sand castle," she ordered.

So it wasn't an igloo. Guess I was wrong.

"Okay," I agreed.

She toddled away. A few minutes later she returned, carrying a bucket.

She carefully poured a little water into her sand castle moat. She dumped the rest on my head.

"Stupid boy!" she squealed, running away.

I rose and shook my wet head like a dog. I felt a strange urge to burst into tears and run to the teacher for help, but I fought it.

Mona stood a few metres away from me, ready to run. "*Nyah nyah!*" she taunted. "Come and get me, Mikey!"

I pushed my wet hair out of my face and stared at Mona.

"You can't catch me!" she called.

What could I do? I had to chase after her.

I began to run. Mona screamed and raced to a tree by the playground fence. Another girl stood there. Was that Ceecee?

She wore thick glasses with pink rims, and underneath, a pink eyepatch.

I'd forgotten about that eyepatch. She'd had to wear it until halfway through first grade.

Mona screamed again and clutched at Ceecee. Ceecee clutched her back and screamed, too.

I stopped in front of the tree. "Don't worry. I won't hurt you," I assured them.

"Yes you will!" Mona squealed. "Help!"

I sat down on the grass to prove I didn't want to hurt them.

"He's hurting us! He's hurting us!" the girls shouted. They unclutched their hands and jumped on top of me.

"Ow!" I cried.

"Hold his arms!" Mona ordered. Ceecee obeyed. Mona started tickling me under the arms.

"Stop it!" I begged. It was torture. "Stop it!"

"No!" Mona cried. "That's what you get for trying to catch us!"

"I . . . didn't . . ." I had trouble getting the words out while she tickled me. "I didn't . . . try to . . ."

"Yes you did!" Mona insisted.

I'd forgotten that Mona used to be so bossy. It made me think twice. If I ever make it back to my real age, I thought, maybe I won't like Mona so much any more.

353

"Please stop," I begged again.

"I'll stop," Mona said. "But only if you promise something."

"What?"

"You have to climb that tree." She pointed to the tree by the fence. "Okay?"

I stared at the tree. Climbing it wouldn't be such a big deal. "Okay," I agreed. "Just get off me!"

Mona stood up. Ceecee let go of my arms.

I climbed to my feet and brushed the grass off my trousers.

"You're scared," Mona taunted.

"I am not!" I replied. What a brat! She was almost as bad as Tara!

Now Mona and Ceecee chanted, "Mikey is scared. Mikey is scared."

I ignored them. I grabbed the lowest branch of the tree and hauled myself up. It was harder than I thought it would be. My four-year-old body wasn't very athletic.

"Mikey is scared. Mikey is scared."

"Shut up!" I yelled down at them. "Can't you see that I'm climbing the stupid tree? It doesn't make sense to tease me about being scared."

They both gave me that blank look Mona had given me before. As if they didn't understand what I was saying.

"Mikey is scared," they chanted again.

I sighed and kept climbing. My hands were so small, it was hard to grip the branches. One of my feet slipped.

Then a terrible thought popped into my head.

Wait a minute.

I shouldn't be doing this.

Isn't playgroup the year I broke my arm?

YEEEEOOOOOOWWWWW!

Morning again.

I yawned and opened my eyes. I shook my left arm, the one I broke climbing that stupid tree the day before.

The arm felt fine. Perfectly normal. Completely healed.

I must have gone back in time again, I thought. That's the good part about this messed-up time thing: I didn't have to wait for my arm to heal.

I wondered how far back I'd gone.

The sun poured in through the window of Tara's—or my—room. It cast a weird shadow across my face: a striped shadow.

I tried to roll out of bed. My body slammed against something.

What was that? I rolled back to look.

Bars!

I was surrounded by bars! Was I in jail?

I tried to sit up so I could see better. It wasn't as

easy as usual. My stomach muscles seemed to have grown weak.

At last I managed to sit up and look around.

I wasn't in jail. I was in a cot!

Crumpled up beside me was my old yellow blankie with the embroidered duck on it. I sat beside a small pile of stuffed animals. I was wearing a tiny white undershirt, and—

Oh, no.

I shut my eyes in horror.

It can't be. Please don't let it be true! I prayed.

I opened my eyes and checked to see if my prayer had come true.

It hadn't.

I was wearing a nappy.

A nappy!

How young am I now? How far back in time did I go? I wondered.

"Are you awake, Mikey?"

Mum came into the room. She looked pretty young. I didn't remember ever seeing her this young before.

"Did you get lots of sleep, sweetie pie?" Mum asked. She clearly expected no answer from me. Instead, she shoved a bottle of juice into my mouth.

Yuck! A bottle!

I pulled it out of my mouth and clumsily threw it down.

Mum picked it up. "No, no," she said patiently.

357

"Bad little Mikey. Drink your bottle now. Come on."

She slid it back into my mouth. I *was* thirsty, so I drank the juice. Drinking from a bottle wasn't that bad, once you got used to it.

Mum left the room. I let the bottle drop.

I had to know how old I was. I had to find out how much time I had left.

I grabbed the bars of the cot and pulled myself to my feet.

Okay, I thought. I can stand.

I took a step. I couldn't control my leg muscles very well. I toddled around the cot.

I can walk, I realized. Unsteadily, but at least I can walk.

I must be about one year old!

I fell just then and banged my head against the side of the cot. Tears welled in my eyes. I started wailing, howling.

Mum ran into the room. "What's the matter, Mikey? What happened?"

She picked me up and started patting me on the back.

I couldn't stop crying. It was really embarrassing.

What am I going to do? I thought desperately. In one night, I went back in time three years!

I'm only one year old now. How old will I be tomorrow?

A little shiver ran down my tiny spine.

I've got to find a way to make time go forward again—today! I told myself.

But what can I do?

I'm not even in playgroup any more.

I'm a baby!

Mum said we were going out. She wanted to dress me. Then she uttered the dreaded words.

"I bet I know what's bothering you, Mikey. You probably need your nappy changed."

"No!" I cried. "No!"

"Oh, yes you do, Mikey. Come on . . ."

I don't like to think about what happened after that. I'd rather block it out of my memory.

I'm sure you understand.

When the worst was over, Mum plopped me down in a playpen—more bars—while she bustled around the house.

I shook a rattle. I batted at a model plane hanging over my head. I watched it spin around.

I pressed buttons on a plastic toy. Different noises came out when I pressed different buttons. A squeak. A honk. A moo.

I was bored out of my mind.

Then Mum picked me up again. She bundled

me into a warm sweater and a dopey little knit cap. Baby blue.

"Want to see Daddy?" she cooed at me. "Want to see Daddy and go shopping?"

"Da-da," I replied.

I'd planned to say, "If you don't take me to Anthony's Antiques, I'll throw myself out of my cot and crack my head open."

But I couldn't talk. It was so frustrating!

Mum carried me out to the car. She strapped me into a baby seat in the back. I tried to say, "Not so tight, Mum!" It came out, "No no no no no!"

"Don't give me a hard time now, Mikey," Mum said sharply. "I know you don't like your car seat, but it's the law." She gave the strap an extra tug.

Then she drove into town.

At least there's a chance, I thought. If we're going to meet Dad, we'll be near the antique store. Maybe, just maybe.

Mum parked the car outside Dad's office building. She unstrapped me from the car seat.

I could move again. But not for long. She pulled a pushchair out of the trunk, unfolded it, and strapped me in.

Being a baby really is like being a prisoner, I thought as she wheeled me across the pavement. I never realized how awful it is!

It was lunchtime. A stream of workers flowed out of the office building. Dad appeared and gave Mum a kiss.

He squatted down to tickle me under the chin. "There's my little boy!" he said.

"Can you say hi to your daddy?" Mum prompted me.

"Hi, Da-da," I gurgled.

"Hi, Mikey," Dad said fondly. But when we stood up, he spoke quietly to Mum, as if I couldn't hear. "Shouldn't he being saying more words by now, honey? Ted Jackson's kid is Mikey's age, and he can say whole sentences. He can say 'lightbulb' and 'kitchen' and 'I want my teddy bear.'"

"Don't start that again," Mum whispered angrily. "Mikey is *not* slow."

I squirmed in my pushchair, fuming. Slow! Who said I was slow?

"I didn't say he was slow, honey," Dad went on. "I only said—"

"Yes you did," Mum insisted. "Yes you did! The other night, when he stuffed those peas up his nose, you said you thought we should have him tested!"

I stuffed peas up my nose? I shuddered.

Sure, stuffing peas up your nose is stupid. But I was only a baby. Wasn't Dad getting carried away?

I thought so.

I wished I could tell them I would turn out all right—at least up to the age of twelve. I mean, I'm no genius, but I get mostly A's and B's.

"Can we discuss this later?" Dad said. "I've only got an hour for lunch. If we're going to find a dining room table, we'd better get moving."

"*You* brought it up," Mum sniffed. She wheeled the pushchair smartly around and began to cross the street. Dad followed us.

I let my eyes rove along the shop windows across the street. An apartment building. A pawnshop. A coffee shop.

Then I found what I was looking for: Anthony's Antiques and Stuff.

My heart leaped. The store still existed! I kept my eyes glued to that sign.

Please take me in there, Mum, I silently prayed. Please please please!

Mum steered me down the street. Past the apartment building. Past the pawnshop. Past the coffee shop.

We stopped in front of Anthony's. Dad stood in front of the window, hands in his pockets, gazing through the glass. Mum and I pulled up beside him.

I couldn't believe it. Finally, after all this time—some good luck!

I stared through the window, searching for it.

The clock.

The window display was set up like an old-fashioned living room. My eyes roamed over the furniture: a wooden bookcase, a fringed table lamp, a Persian rug, an overstuffed armchair, and a clock . . . a table clock. Not the cuckoo clock.

Not the right clock.

My heart sank back to its normal low spot in my chest.

It figures, I thought. Here I am, at the antique shop, at last.

And the clock isn't here.

I felt like crying.

I could have cried, too. Easily.

After all, I was a baby. People expected me to cry.

But I didn't. Even though I looked like a baby, I was a twelve-year-old inside. I still had my pride.

Dad stepped to the door and held it open for Mum and me. Mum pushed me inside. I sat strapped into the pushchair.

The shop was jammed with old furniture. A chubby man in his forties strolled down the aisle towards us.

Behind him, down at the end of the aisle, in a corner at the back of the shop, I saw it. The clock. *The* clock.

A squeal of excitement popped out of me. I began to rock in my pram. I was so close!

"May I help you?" the man asked Mum and Dad.

"We're looking for a dining room table," Mum told him.

I had to get out of that pushchair. I had to get to that clock.

I rocked harder, but it was no good. I was strapped in. "Let me out of this thing!" I shouted.

Mum and Dad turned to look at me. "What's he saying?" Dad asked.

"It sounded like 'La ma la ma'," the shopkeeper suggested.

I rocked harder than ever and screamed.

"He hates his pushchair," Mum explained. She leaned down and unbuckled the straps. "I'll hold him for a few minutes. Then he'll quieten down."

I waited until she held me in her arms. Then I screamed again and wriggled as hard as I could.

Dad's face reddened. "Michael, what is wrong with you?"

"Down! Down!" I yelled.

"All right," Mum muttered, setting me down on the floor. "Now please stop screaming."

I quietened down immediately. I tested my wobbly, chubby little legs. They wouldn't get me far, but they were all I had to work with.

"Keep an eye on him," the shopkeeper warned. "A lot of this stuff is breakable."

Mum grabbed my hand. "Come on, Mikey. Let's go look at some tables."

She tried to lead me to a corner of the shop where several wooden tables stood. I whined and squirmed, hoping to get away. Her grip was too tight.

"Mikey, *shh*," she said.

I let her drag me to the tables. I glanced up at the cuckoo clock. It was almost noon.

At noon, I knew, the cuckoo would pop out. It was my only chance to grab the bird and turn it around.

I tugged on Mum's hand. She tightened her grip.

"What do you think of this one, honey?" Dad asked her, rubbing his hand along a dark wood table.

"I think that wood's too dark for our chairs, Herman," Mum said. Another table caught her eye. As she moved towards it, I tried to slip my hand out of hers. No go.

I toddled after her to the second table. I shot another glance at the clock. The minute hand moved.

Two minutes to twelve.

"We can't be too picky, honey," Dad said. "The Bergers are coming over Saturday night—two days from now—for a dinner party. We can't have a dinner party without a dining room table!"

367

"I *know* that, dear. But there's no point in buying a table we don't like."

Dad's voice began to rise. Mum's mouth got that hard, set look to it.

Aha. A fight. This was my chance.

Dad was shouting. "Why don't we just spread a blanket out on the floor and make them eat there? We'll call it a picnic!"

Mum finally relaxed her grip on my hand.

I slipped away and toddled as fast as I could towards the clock.

The clock's minute hand moved again.

I toddled faster.

I heard my parents shouting at each other. "I won't buy an ugly table, and that's that!" Mum cried.

Please don't let them notice me, I prayed. Not yet.

I reached the cuckoo clock at last. I stood in front of it and stared up at the clock.

The cuckoo's window was far above me, out of reach.

The minute hand clicked again. The clock's gong sounded.

The cuckoo's window slid open. The cuckoo popped out.

It cuckooed once.

It cuckooed twice.

I stared up at it, helpless.

A twelve-year-old boy trapped in a baby's body.

I stared grimly up at the clock.

Somehow, I had to reach that cuckoo.

Somehow, I *had* to turn it around.

Cuckoo! Cuckoo!

Three, four.

I knew that once it reached twelve, I was doomed.

The cuckoo bird would disappear.

And so would my last chance to save myself.

In a day or so, I would disappear. Disappear for ever.

Frantic, I glanced around for a ladder, a stool, anything.

The closest thing was a chair.

I toddled over to the chair and pushed it towards the clock. It moved a few centimetres.

I leaned, putting all my weight into it. I figured I weighed about twenty pounds.

But it was enough. The chair began to slide across the floor.

Cuckoo! Cuckoo! Five, six.

I shoved the chair up against the clock. The seat of the chair came up to my chin.

I tried to pull myself up on to the seat. My arms were too weak.

I planted a baby shoe against the chair leg. I boosted myself up. I grabbed a spindle at the back of the chair and heaved my body on to the seat.

I made it!

Cuckoo! Cuckoo! Seven, eight.

I got to my knees. I got to my feet.

I reached up to grab the cuckoo. I stretched as tall as I could.

Cuckoo! Cuckoo! Nine, ten.

Reaching, reaching.

Then I heard the shopkeeper shout, "Somebody grab that baby!"

I heard pounding footsteps.

They were running to get me.

I strained to reach the cuckoo. Just another inch . . .

Cuckoo!

Eleven.

Mum grabbed me. She lifted me up.

For one second, the cuckoo flashed within my reach.

I grasped it and turned the head around.

Cuckoo!

Twelve.

The cuckoo slid back into the clock, facing the right way.

Forward.

I wriggled out of Mum's arms, landing on the chair.

"Mikey, what's got into you?" she cried. She tried to grab me again.

I dodged her. I reached around to the side of the clock.

I saw the little dial that told the year. I felt for the button that controlled it. I could just reach it, standing on the chair.

I slammed my hand on the button, carefully watching the years whiz by.

I heard the shopkeeper yelling, "Get that baby away from my clock!"

Mum grabbed me again, but I screamed. I screamed so loudly, it startled her. She let her hands drop.

"Mikey, let go of that!" Dad ordered.

I took my hand off the button. The dial showed the right year. The present year. The year I turned twelve.

Mum made another grab for me. This time I let her pick me up.

It doesn't matter what happens now, I thought. Either the clock will work, and I'll go back to being twelve again . . .

. . . or else it won't work. And then what?

Then I'll disappear. Vanish in time. For ever.

I waited.

"I'm so sorry," Dad said to the shopkeeper. "I hope the baby didn't damage the clock."

The muscles in my neck tensed.

Nothing was happening. Nothing.

I waited another minute.

373

The shopkeeper inspected the clock. "Everything seems okay," he told Dad. "But he's changed the year. I'll have to change it back."

"NO!" I wailed. "No! Don't!"

"That boy could use a little discipline, if you ask me," the shopkeeper said.

He reached his hand around the side of the clock and started to set back the year.

"Nooo!" I wailed. "Nooo!"

That's it, I realized. I'm doomed. I'm a goner.

But the shopkeeper never touched the button.

A bright white light flashed. I felt dizzy, stunned. I blinked. And blinked again.

Several seconds passed before I could see anything.

I felt cool, damp air. I smelled at a musty odour. A garage smell.

"Michael? Do you like it?" Dad's voice.

I blinked. My eyes adjusted. I saw Dad and Mum. Looking older. Looking *normal*.

We were standing in the garage. Dad was holding a shiny new 21-speed bike.

Mum frowned. "Michael, are you feeling all right?"

They were giving me the bike. It was my birthday!

The clock worked! I'd brought myself back to the present!

Almost to the present. Up to my twelfth birthday.

Close enough.

I felt so happy, I thought I'd explode.

I threw myself at Mum and hugged her hard. Then I hugged Dad.

"Wow," Dad gushed. "I guess you really *do* like the bike!"

I grinned. "I love it!" I exclaimed. "I love everything! I love the whole world!"

Mainly, I loved being twelve again. I could walk! I could talk! I could ride the bus by myself!

Whoa! Wait a minute, I thought. It's my birthday.

Don't tell me I have to live through it *again*.

I tensed my shoulders and steeled myself for the horrible day to come.

It's worth it, I told myself. It's worth it if it means time will go forward again, the way it's supposed to.

I knew too well what would happen next.

Tara.

She'd try to get on my bike. The bike would fall over and get scratched.

Okay, Tara, I thought. I'm ready. Come and do your worst.

I waited.

Tara didn't come.

In fact, she didn't seem to be around at all.

She wasn't in the garage. No sign of her.

Mum and Dad *oohed* and *ahhed* over the bike. They didn't act as if anything was wrong. Or anyone was missing.

"Where's Tara?" I asked them.

They looked up.

"Who?" They stared at me.

"Did you invite her to your party?" Mum asked. "I don't remember sending an invitation to a Tara."

Dad grinned at me. "Tara? Is that some girl you have a crush on, Michael?"

"No," I answered, turning red.

It was as if they'd never heard of Tara. Never heard of their own daughter.

"You'd better go upstairs and get ready for your party, Michael," Mum suggested. "The kids will be here soon."

"Okay." I stumbled into the house, dazed.

"Tara?" I called.

Silence.

Could she be hiding somewhere?

I searched through the house. Then I checked her room. I threw open the door. I expected to see a messy, all-pink girl's room with a white canopy bed.

Instead, I saw two twin beds, neatly made with plaid covers. A chair. An empty closet. No personal stuff.

Not Tara's room.

A guest room.

Wow. I was amazed.

No Tara. Tara doesn't exist.

How did that happen?

I wandered into the den, looking for the cuckoo clock.

It wasn't there.

For a second, I felt a shock of fear. Then I calmed down.

Oh, yeah, I remembered. We don't have the clock yet. Not on my birthday. Dad bought it a couple of days later.

But I still didn't understand. What had happened to my little sister? Where was Tara?

My friends arrived for the party. We played CDs and ate tortilla chips. Ceecee pulled me into a corner and whispered that Mona had a crush on me.

Wow. I glanced at Mona. She turned a little pink and glanced away, shyly.

Tara wasn't there to embarrass me. It made a big difference.

My friends had all brought presents. I actually opened them myself. No Tara to open my presents before I got to them.

At cake time, I carried the cake into the dining room and set it in the middle of the table. No problem. I didn't fall and make a fool out of myself.

378

Because Tara wasn't there to trip me.

It was the greatest birthday party I'd ever had. It was probably the greatest *day* I'd ever lived— because Tara wasn't there to ruin it.

I could get used to this, I thought.

A few days later, the cuckoo clock was delivered to our house.

"Isn't it great?" Dad gushed, as he had the first time. "Anthony sold me the clock cheap. He said he'd discovered a tiny flaw on it."

The flaw. I'd almost forgotten about it.

We still didn't know what it was. But I couldn't help wondering if it had something to do with Tara's disappearance.

Maybe the clock didn't work perfectly in some way? Maybe it had somehow left Tara behind?

I hardly dared to touch the clock. I didn't want to set off any more weird time trips.

But I had to know what had happened.

I carefully studied the face of the clock again, and all the decorations. Then I stared at the dial that showed the year.

It was properly set at the current year.

Without really thinking about it, I scanned twelve places down the dial to find the year I was born.

There it was.

Then I scanned my eyes back up the dial. 1984. 1985. 1986. 1987. 1989 . . .

Wait a second.

Didn't I just skip a year?

I checked the dates again.

Nineteen-eighty-eight was missing. There was no 1988 on the dial.

And 1988 was the year Tara was born!

"Dad!" I cried. "I found the flaw! Look—there's a year missing on the dial."

Dad patted me on the back. "Good job, son! Wow, isn't that funny?"

To him it was just a funny mistake.

He had no idea his daughter had never been born.

I suppose there's some way to go back in time and get her.

I guess I probably ought to do that.

And I will.

Really.

One of these days.

Maybe.